"I'm not going to sleep with you," Nick insisted

Not to be deterred, Serena reached out and lazily ran her hand over his leg. "Sure. Okay."

Nick jumped back as if he'd been burned. "I'm serious. You're wasting your time here, Serena. You can report back to AJ that you came, you saw and you didn't conquer. The bet's still on."

She stood and stepped closer to him. "Fine." Then, before he could stop her, she slipped her index fingers into the edge of his pants, feeling a rush at the warm satin of his skin against the backs of her fingers. "But Nick, fooling around isn't sleeping. Can't we still play?" She didn't have to work at imbuing her voice with a low huskiness.

He grabbed her wrists and set her away from him. "It's time for you to leave, Serena."

But she couldn't. Even though she'd love to run screaming from the room and leave behind the fire ignited by the brief touch of his hands, she had a job to do. She shook her head and scraped her fingernail down his chest. "But I just got here. We haven't even had any fun yet." She paused. "And Nick, I've heard you're *lots* of fun...."

Blaze™

Dear Reader,

I knew when I first introduced Nick O'Malley in his big
brother's story, *Really Hot!*, that he was special. But I wasn't
prepared for the onslaught of reader mail I got asking for
Nick's story. And since I always listen and try to deliver when
I can, here is Nick's Blazing tale....

But not just any woman would do for Nick. She had to be
someone different, someone special. And when Serena Riggs,
a tough undercover cop, breezed into my imagination, I knew
Nick had met his match.

It's one of my favorite setups in a romance—putting together
two people who are intellectually the worst possible choice for
one another, but ultimately just what the other needs. And they
need each other quite a bit in this story....

I hope you enjoy Nick and Serena's grand adventure. I would
love to hear from you. Check me out and e-mail me at my
Web site, www.jenniferlabrecque.com, or snail mail me at
P.O. Box 298, Hiram, GA 30141.

Happy reading,

Jennifer LaBrecque

Books by Jennifer LaBrecque

HARLEQUIN BLAZE

HARLEQUIN TEMPTATION

ANTICIPATION
Jennifer LaBrecque

HARLEQUIN®

TORONTO • NEW YORK • LONDON
AMSTERDAM • PARIS • SYDNEY • HAMBURG
STOCKHOLM • ATHENS • TOKYO • MILAN • MADRID
PRAGUE • WARSAW • BUDAPEST • AUCKLAND

Acknowledgment

Thanks to the Boston Police Department for the inspiration.
All the inaccuracies are strictly my own.

Dedication

To Robert, my Massachusetts-born hero.
I'm glad you decided to stay.

ISBN 0-373-79232-8

ANTICIPATION

Copyright © 2006 by Jennifer LaBrecque.

www.eHarlequin.com

Printed in U.S.A.

1

"I GET OFF OF work in two hours." Cherry, a new waitress, placed the wings and a beer pitcher in the table's center. The food and drinks were for everyone, but the sultry look was for Nick only.

Nick O'Malley smiled back at her but didn't comment. Cherry stood, blocking the ball game. Obviously the regular staff at Dougal's Sports Bar and Grill hadn't taught Cherry the cardinal rule of waitressing in a sports bar: no blocking the big screen. Dougal's wasn't Boston's finest or oldest, but Nick and his buddies had idled away many afternoons and evenings there in the past nine years since they'd reached legal drinking age. Cherry finally left, casting an inviting glance over her shoulder on her way to the kitchen.

"Man, you suck. You don't even have to try to pick up chicks," AJ groused and reached for the wing basket, shaking his blond crew-cut head in disgust.

The room groaned in chorus as Donovan struck out Perez…bases loaded…third out at the top of the ninth. The Red Sox had shot *that* game to hell.

"It's gotten even worse since you hit every trashy newspaper in the country." AJ didn't let it go. "Amazing. You get caught embezzling half a million, your big brother goes on two reality shows to help you come up with the money you owe, the press gets wind of it and—*bam*—you're famous."

And he'd rather AJ not bring it up. It hadn't exactly been his finest moment. His serious lapse in judgment had affected his whole family. He'd felt the worst about humiliating his parents. The look in their eyes had shattered him. It was something he lived with every day. They hadn't been aghast as much as accepting. Irresponsible Nick had struck again.

Not a day went by that he didn't think about it and rue what he'd done. His mom and dad had stood by him, but told him he had to take responsibility for his actions. He was determined to go one better. He'd never be his older brother, Rourke—talk about a tough act to follow—but he'd finally figured out that being Nick didn't mean landing himself in jail. And standing in Rourke's shadow was something he could choose to do or not.

Although, in a fatalistic kind of way, he wondered if it wasn't supposed to happen and play out the way it had. Rourke had met the woman of his dreams, the associate producer for the two reality shows he'd been on. Portia and Rourke were now happily married and Rourke had bonded like glue with his stepson. Maybe their paths would never have crossed if Nick hadn't screwed up. And maybe Nick wouldn't have grown up and figured out a lot about himself and life in general. One thing for sure, he was never going to get himself into another scrape that embarrassed his family and required Rourke to rescue him.

Nick knew he was lucky he hadn't done jail time for his crime. Lance Gleeson had declined to press charges as long as the money was returned with interest. Nick was also eternally grateful that the women of the world didn't seem to hold it against him, even though it was sort of weird that not only did they not mind, they almost seemed to like it.

"It's gotten better. I think my fifteen minutes of infamy have passed." The latest celebrity couple breakup and another headline proclaiming aliens had visited the White House, and he was yesterday's news. Thank goodness.

"Yeah. In a whole month no one's mobbed us when we've been out with Nicky," Tim said. He was the peacemaker and the only married one in the group. He agreed with whomever was making a point at the time, whether it contradicted what he'd just said or not, a trait that went a long way with his wife, Marsha.

"Chicks have always dug him," AJ said.

Nick shrugged. He liked women and they seemed to like him. It worked. AJ wasn't a bad-looking guy and he made decent money as a site foreman for his father's construction company, but he had an attitude problem that women picked up on. *Chicks.* "I've been trying to tell you for years, that's your problem. They're not chicks. They're women. They know you think of them as chicks."

"Man's got a point," Tim said, refilling his beer. Nick held out his empty mug and Tim did the honors. "Marsha says 'chick' is demeaning."

AJ shook his head. "Nah. That's not it at all." AJ poured extra hot sauce on his wings. Nick had tried one of AJ's wings several years ago. Personally, he thought there was a lot to be said for still being able to feel your tongue when eating. Nick picked up a mild drummette and bit into it while AJ rambled on. AJ was fond of the sound of his own voice. "Nicky's addicted to women. They sense it and they want to provide his fix."

What? AJ was—

"You're full of it," Matt said, dipping a carrot stick in blue-cheese dressing. Between carrying a few extra pounds and early male-pattern baldness, Matt definitely looked the oldest of the four, even though he was six months younger.

AJ eyed the plastic basket of carrots and celery. "Your dick's gonna fall off eating that. You should try some real man food." Cousins as well as friends, AJ and Matt constantly gave one another a hard time.

Matt feigned surprise. "Damn. That's what happened to you, man? Aunt Celeste fed you a carrot and your pecker dropped off? All these years we thought you'd just been shortchanged at birth." He munched his carrot.

"Blow me." AJ stabbed his chicken bone in Matt's direction. "And I'm telling you, Nick's addicted to chicks."

Nick thunked his empty mug onto the scarred wood, thoroughly enjoying himself. "I'm not addicted to women."

"Sure you are." AJ smirked. "Name one time since junior high that you've gone longer than two weeks without a girlfriend."

"There was…" Wait, *that* hadn't been a week, but what about the time… "Yeah, when I had that emergency appendectomy and couldn't take Melissa Frecht to the dance and she dumped me."

"Sorry, loser. Remember the girl who started bringing your assignments over and doing them for you?"

Martha Crawford.

"Oh. Yeah. Okay. But that doesn't prove anything."

"Nicky wants proof." AJ grinned and hoisted his beer at Matt and Tim with a smirk. "You and Trish have been quits for what, three days now?"

"Something like that." Trish had wanted a ring, as in engagement ring, for her thirtieth birthday. Nick had been thinking more along the lines of a box of chocolates. She hadn't liked his idea and he sure hadn't gone for hers. Seeing Rourke and his sister-in-law together had actually left him discontented, wanting more than he had. But Trish wasn't the woman he'd consider growing old beside.

"Five hundred bucks says you can't go without a woman for thirty days," AJ said. He bet on everything.

And Nick usually took him up on it. "Piece of cake," Nick shrugged. He could do this and it went along with his new vow of being more responsible.

Matt whistled through his teeth. "Thirty days is a long time, Nick."

"Especially for you." Tim looked at Nick in apology.

"What?" Tim shifted like the wind. "You guys have no faith in me?" Obviously he needed to prove himself as the new and improved Nick to his buddies.

"You…thirty days…no women…" Matt looked at Tim, who grimaced. Matt glanced back at Nick and shook his head. "Sorry, dude."

AJ smirked. "Money talks, bullshit walks."

Nick leaned back in his chair. "We'll see. Define *going without*. Are we talking no dates? Phone calls? Kisses? Nothing?"

AJ reached for another wing. "Second thoughts? This looking a little harder than you thought?"

"It'll be a walk in the park." Maybe an understatement, but he could do this. For his own self-respect he had to do this. It was proof of the new direction in his life. Plus, five hundred bucks would leave a big whole in his pocket.

"How many beers have you had?" Matt asked.

Two? Maybe three? "Not that many." He looked across the table at AJ. "Now are you gonna lay out the rules or are you rethinking putting your money where your mouth is?"

AJ grinned and Nick didn't bother to tell him he had a chunk of chicken stuck in his front teeth. "I'm putting my money on a sure thing. No dates. No kissing. No copping a feel. Absolutely no sex of any kind and, yeah, that includes phone sex, hand jobs and blow jobs."

Matt winced. "That's harsh, AJ."

"You're being pretty rough on him," Tim said.

Nick swallowed. Obviously his three buds thought he'd cave before he even got in the game. "Not a problem."

AJ laughed. "Right. This is gonna be the easiest five hundred bucks I ever made."

He'd known AJ a long time, ever since the four of them had played Little League together. Nick had a few rules of his own to throw out, based on how well he knew AJ. "You can't screw around with me and send women my way. That's cheating."

"Wrong. All's fair in love and war, isn't it, boys?" AJ glanced across the table at Matt and Tim.

"Man's got a point," Tim said. You couldn't count on Tim to back you up in a tight spot.

Matt polished off the last carrot stick. "Sounds fair to me."

"Majority rules." AJ hoisted his beer in a mock toast. "A man on a deserted island can go without a beer, but put a pitcher in front of him and then you know what he's made of."

"WAIT TILL YOU GET a load of this, Riggs." Brian Bennigan grinned and nodded toward the captain's office as Serena Riggs made her way through the bullpen of Boston's 151st precinct, located in the less-than-scenic heart of Boston's most crime-ridden area.

Joe Pantoni tossed in his two-cents' worth. "It's right up your alley, Riggs. If you can't catch Malone with this one, we'll check and see if you can get on desk duty."

"Last I heard, you had dibs on that spot, Pantyoni," she said with her own smirk as she passed his desk. Being busted down from detective to desk clerk was a running department joke.

"Hey, Riggs, if you need to get in a little practice, Bennigan says he's available. He's got a *little* something in common with your perp," Mike Harding piped up. Bennigan gave him the finger from across the room.

Steve Shea laughed with the rest of them, but withheld comment.

"Stuff it, boys," Serena said good-naturedly, dropping her purse on her desk. They were a mouthy, but essentially harmless, group of guys.

She, Bennigan, Pantoni and Harding had all been knocking around the 151st since their rookie days. Bit by bit, the men had insinuated themselves into the fabric of her life.

They and their families had had her on rotation for the past five years. Mike and Becca Harding commandeered her at Christmas. Pantoni's wife, Francesca, always insisted Serena join their enormous and enormously loud extended family for Thanksgiving—although that would change this year. Francesca had decided she'd had enough of a cop's lousy hours and the lousier pay, along with the gut-eating stress of being a cop's wife. She and Joe were locked in mortal urban combat, commonly known as divorce. And Bennigan, the clichéd but oh-so-sweet third-generation Irish-American cop, dragged her along for St. Patrick's Day, a holiday that ran a close third to Christmas and Thanksgiving in Boston.

She razzed them that they only had her over so she'd bring dessert—she could kick some pastry butt. Cannolis and tiramisu for the Pantonis, the Hardings were particularly fond of her éclairs and amaretto cheesecake, and she always baked several loaves of Irish soda bread and a chocolate mousse with Irish cream topping for the Bennigan clan. She liked to bake and it made her feel less of a charity case. Unlike her first several years in Boston, the past five had never found her alone on a family holiday, thanks to "the boys" and their families.

"PMS," Pantoni surmised in a stage whisper.

"Definitely hormonal," Bennigan agreed.

She gave them the finger behind her back as she eased into the captain's office.

"Today's your lucky day," Harlan Worth announced as Serena closed his office door behind her.

"Yeah. So I gathered running the gauntlet." She slumped into the chair in front of his beat-up desk and sipped the sludge disguised as coffee, still half a cup away from being fully humanoid. Where was it written that police station coffee had to be so bad? She vowed she'd never sleep through another alarm again and not have time to make her own coffee at home.

Worth steepled his fingers. "We've got a lead on Slick Nick for you."

Finally. She'd been chasing Nick Malone, a money-laundering suspect, for months. However, she'd wait until she heard the particulars of the lead to decide whether it had validity. "Let's hear it." She pulled a small notepad out of her purse. She wrote everything down. More than once she'd reviewed her notes and found some obscure detail or minutia that had proven to be key.

"Got to love your enthusiasm, Riggs."

Chasing dead ends had taught her not to get too hopeful. "I'll see if I think it's something to get excited about."

"Seems Slick Nick dumped a girlfriend and you know how you women get." She let the comment pass. If she took exception to every sexist comment uttered in the 151st, she'd be a raving lunatic. Besides, Harlan, despite his bluster, was one of the nicest men she'd ever met. He'd been married to Nancy Worth for over forty years and still worshipped the ground the woman walked on. "She's selling her stud-muffin down the river."

Stud-muffin? Harlan was stuck in the eighties. Serena focused on the rest of what he'd said. Depending on just how pissed off they were, ex-girlfriends could provide a wealth of info. Maybe this *was* something to get excited about.

She knew Nick Malone was a little over six feet with short, dark hair, blue eyes, and a medium build. That had only narrowed it down to over half the men in greater Boston. She needed a photo and a means of positive ID. The guy had been smart enough never to get caught or arrested. No fingerprints, no photo ID, and he went by several aliases. "Please tell me we have a photo."

"We have a photo." Harlan pushed it across the desk in her direction. "For what it's worth." The photo was out of focus, the man in the picture little more than a blur, with no discernable features, other than dark, short hair.

"Oh." Yep. As disappointing as every other lead in this case. She drained the cup and bit back a grimace. She was saving every dollar for a down payment on a town house, but she might have to break down and buy a decent cup of coffee at the nearby coffee shop when she overslept. This stuff was either going to kill her or put hair on her chest—both bad options.

Harlan flipped through his notes, which Serena knew was unnecessary. The man possessed an amazing memory. "According to the girlfriend, he's a top-notch dresser. Likes nice clothes. Said he's obsessed with them ocean movies."

Huh? "Beach movies?"

"Nah. *Ocean's Eleven* and *Ocean's Twelve*. She says he wants to be like that Clooney guy."

Serena cracked a smile. "There are worse men to want to be like, although I personally think Matt Damon's the looker in that lot."

"You seen the movies?"

"Yeah." The ending in the second one, *Ocean's Twelve*, irritated the heck out of her. "So, we've got a perp who fancies himself a master criminal."

"Hey, at least he's got professional ambition." Harlan unwrapped a Twinkie. "Breakfast of champions." He took a bite and swallowed with minimal chewing. Watching Harlan eat reminded her why she was still single. Men could be real pigs. That and you needed to trust them to marry them. "We also know that our boy has a tattoo."

"That works." Finally something to really smile about. A perp could alter haircut and color, pop in colored contacts, change the way he dressed, but it was hard to get rid of a tattoo or a scar. "Arm? Neck? Chest? Back?"

"This is good." Harlan grinned, looking like one of Santa's elves gone bad with his full, round face, slightly pointed ears and a blob of cream filling at the corner of his mouth. She made a sign and he swiped off the cream. "It's on his ass."

Serena rolled her eyes. No wonder the boys had been in rare form this morning. "That's great. To make a positive ID I've got to yank this guy's pants down?"

Harlan chased the Twinkie with a slurp of coffee sludge. "You could try asking him nicely. According to the girlfriend, he's quite a looker, but she says he's a tiny mite when it comes to the johnson—course that could just be the woman-scorned thing."

Serena laughed. That must be the *little* something Bennigan had in common with Malone. "That's just great! This'll make for some interesting conversation. *Excuse me, you look like someone I know. In fact, you remind me of Danny Ocean. But I need to know, do you have a tattoo on your butt and a little penis?"*

"Hey, it'll guarantee a positive ID." Harlan smirked. "Another little tidbit for when you're trying to get those pants down to check out the tattoo—your boy likes a good spanking. You might want to dust off your dominatrix outfit."

Sometimes she just found out more than she wanted or needed to know about people. Being in a job where she was surrounded by the worst of society was often demoralizing. "I didn't need to know that."

Harlan wagged a stubby finger at her across the

desk. "It might come in handy. You've got to work on always having a backup plan, Riggs. She says he's particularly partial to one of those little riding whips with the split leather on the end."

"Jesus. Was there anything she *didn't* tell you?"

"She was singing like a bird." Harlan grinned.

"Please, tell me we've got an address." Slick Nick was a shadow man. She hadn't been able to find out where he lived. An address would be a huge plus. That she would definitely smile about.

"Sorry, Toots. You aren't *that* lucky today. She said they always went to her place or a motel and they always took a cab. But, she did say he has an important meeting at that hotel near the airport, The Barrister. He's going to be there for a three-day meeting from the twenty-fourth until the twenty-sixth. Just think, you can spank him till he talks and he'll like it."

Okay, it looked like dominatrix was about to be added to her repertoire. Serena was the department "go to" girl when light undercover was required. She liked it and she excelled at it. She'd handle the dominatrix thing without a problem.

Color her cynical, but this seemed like a surfeit of information where before they'd only had one dead-end after another. "How do you know she's not setting us up? That's a lot of information for her to know."

"Nuh-uh. She's setting *him* up, big-time. Apparently he thought she was just a dumb blonde and didn't really go to any trouble to hide his day planner. So she found it and took a look."

Serena grinned. "I like the sound of this woman." Well, except for her poor judgment in dating a crook. Growing up with a petty criminal for a father had left Serena with zero tolerance and had been a major influence on her decision to be a cop. Criminals were criminals—bottom line. And women who had anything to do with law-breakers were almost as bad as the men themselves.

If Serena's mother had left her good-for-nothing father, they would've still been poor, but at least they could've claimed a little dignity. Pretty damn hard to have dignity when your old man was in and out of prison all the time and your mother lied to cover for him.

Serena had bailed when she hit eighteen. A high-school graduate with thirty-two hundred bucks in her pocket, saved from working nights and weekends, she'd tried to get her mother to come with her. Her mother had stayed because, according to Mom, Serena's dad needed her when he got of jail. Again.

Serena had shaken Cleveland's dirt from her feet, headed east and, even though she talked regularly with her mom, she'd never gone back. She couldn't face the squalor and her mom's resigned hopefulness. She definitely wasn't interested in her father's lies that this time he was going straight.

Becoming a cop had been Serena's way of denouncing everything her father stood for. Plus, her father truly hated cops. Her job might keep her in contact with criminals and all the emotional dysfunction that went with a criminal's lifestyle, but she was fighting all that instead of living it. "The girlfriend's more than a blond bimbo. Bad news for Slick Nick. Good news for *moi*."

"Don't you want to know what kind of tattoo he has on his ass?" The elf-gone-bad's eyes fairly danced with mischief.

Serena blew a strand of hair out of her eyes. She wanted to grow her hair out, but she might not make it through this growing out stage. And PMS just made it worse. She should come with a warning today: Bad Hair Day, PMS Bloating and a License to Carry Concealed. "I'm thinking there is a limited number of men that fit his general description with any kind of tattoo on their butts, but sure, go ahead. I can tell you're dying to spill it. And doubtless the guys all know already. They were in rare form this morning." Secrets in the station just didn't happen.

"Right cheek. It's a heart with MOM inside it." Harlan cracked up. "Apparently that's the side he prefers for his spanking."

"I TOLD YOU NOT to call me before ten in the morning," "Slick Nick" Malone said into his cell phone. Couldn't a guy get a decent night's sleep?

"Wake up and pay attention, Nicky, because

I'm beginning to think you could fuck up a wet dream."

Nick curled his fist around the phone. One day he'd find out who this cop was and then he'd pop him. For now it was useful having a guy on the inside. But sooner or later, he'd make him, and then the voice on the other end was history.

The cop was always so foulmouthed. His language deeply offended Nick. But Nick thought his cop-in-a-pocket knew that and went out of his way to needle him with it. When he was a kid, Nick's neighborhood had been a dump—graffiti-covered buildings, foul language not only spouted all around him but spray painted for the world to see. Back them, no matter how many times he'd washed his hands or how clean he'd tried to keep his clothes, he'd always felt the filth of his surroundings. Eventually he'd managed to put the neighborhood behind him and all it represented. He wore nice clothes. Kept his language clean. Stayed in nice places. Ate at nice restaurants.

The woman in the hotel bed next to him, Susie maybe, was still asleep, her mouth gaping open slightly. Phone in hand, Nick slid out of bed, still naked from the night before, and crossed the room, then closed the bedroom door behind him. He stretched out on the suite's love seat, the brocade upholstery rough against his back and bare butt.

"What are you talking about?"

The voice laughed, an ugly sound so early in

the morning. "Your girlfriend or should I say ex-girlfriend, Debi, has been flapping her trap."

Apprehension grabbed him by the balls and squeezed. He swung his feet to the floor and sat up. "What?"

"She visited the station and filled us in on all kinds of little nifty details like who you're meeting and where and when."

Nick stood and stalked over to the window. Fury roiled through him. "She's dead."

He hated it when he lost control and said stuff like that. Another reason to kill her. Jesus. He rested his forehead on the chilled glass of the window and closed his eyes.

"Nick, Nick, Nick. Don't even think about breathing hard in her direction." The hated voice sighed. "You know, it really annoys me when I have to think for both of us. If she turns up dead or missing or even with a broken fingernail, game's up, bright boy. My people will figure out the information was leaked and then you and I are out of business and—who knows?—I just might be the one arresting your punk ass." That laugh grated on Nick's nerves like nails scraping a chalkboard. "And you'd never know it was me. So, listen up, loser, you don't touch Debi Majette. Next time you want to dump a girlfriend, make it a body, before she talks to us. Get your shit together."

Jo-Jo would have his head for this. His uncle Jo-Jo had been the one to offer him the opportunity to move beyond the 'hood, and Jo-Jo could just as easily send him back. Christ. He tamped down his panic. But it was fixable. Definitely fixable. He just needed a few minutes to think this through without the cop hanging on the line.

"We'll move O'Malley into place," Nick said, thinking aloud. "I'll meet my contacts elsewhere and we'll send O'Malley to The Barrister on those dates. It's a little sooner than we'd planned, but it should work."

"You're sure O'Malley doesn't suspect anything?"

Nick curled his lip. Even though he'd never met him, he despised Nick O'Malley and all the others like him out there. He'd read about O'Malley's background in the papers. No graffiti-covered sidewalks in O'Malley's childhood. No hookers on the corner across from the drug dealers. No, O'Malley was one of those laid-back lucky gimps who always landed on his feet. He led a charmed life. "Doesn't have a clue. He's so used to lady luck smiling on him, he never questioned the job offer."

Once Jo-Jo had found out the cops were hot on Nick's tail, he'd heard O'Malley's story in the news and come up with a brilliant idea. Hire O'Malley to work in one of Jo-Jo's secondary companies. Let him get comfortable, set him up and then let him take the fall as Slick Nick. O'Malley didn't look like him, but they were close to the same build, nearly the same weight and about the same age. Every tabloid had carried the story that O'Malley had committed a crime, yet never done time. It was a beautiful plan. It'd take the heat off of him and O'Malley could enjoy the creature comforts of the state pen—and get a taste of what if felt like when lady luck spit in your face.

"Except now we all know you have a tattoo on your ass and he doesn't," the cop said.

Nick couldn't think with this jerk hanging on the other end of the line. "I'll figure something out and take care of it. Thanks for the heads-up," Nick said. He hated thanking this piece of scum for anything.

"No problem…as long as you pay up. You know the deal."

Nick watched the snarl of traffic on the street below. The little people rushing to and fro for their nine-to-five jobs. Pathetic slobs.

"Yeah. I know the deal." Cash deposited into a numbered bank account.

"You know, I'm feeling generous today, so I'll throw this in as a freebie, won't even charge you extra for the info. Everyone in the 151st not only knows you have a tattoo on your ass, they also know you get off on a good spanking."

Nick fisted his hand in the curtain.

The voice on the other end of the line laughed. "And the Debster says you've got a little dick. That's a shame. Size really does matter."

Giving way to his fury, Nick flipped the phone closed, cutting off the hateful laughter on the other end. He threw it against the wall and dragged in a deep breath.

One day. One day that bitch would pay for that. The same as that nameless, faceless cop.

2

"TWENTY-THREE DAYS DOWN, seven left to go. You're never going to make it," AJ said.

"I'm practically home free." Okay, so maybe he'd underestimated just how prominent a factor women were in his life. But it hadn't been as hard as Nick had anticipated, despite his buddies going out of their way to make it as difficult as possible. AJ and Matt had sent women his way left and right over the past twenty-three days. Matt had thrown a party, complete with lots of single, available, hot women. Oddly enough, none of them had even seriously tempted Nick. He didn't expect it to be easy, but seven more days was doable.

"Home free, my ass. You're gonna break before you manage another week." AJ laughed. "You look ready to break now."

"Man's got a point." Tim eyed him across a half-eaten Rueben, Dougal's special of the day. "You look wound pretty tight."

Nick forked a home fry. "You only think that because AJ's brainwashed you."

Matt tipped his stool back on two legs. "No

one's brainwashed me. You should have seen your face when Polly squeezed behind your chair."

"What did you expect? Polly's got these big…" Maybe he was in worse shape than he'd thought, he couldn't say the word *breasts* without choking. "You know…and she—they brushed against my back." And he wouldn't even mention how good she'd smelled and how sweet her breasts had felt against his back. He didn't doubt that AJ had slipped her—the prettiest waitress with the biggest tatas—a twenty to squeeze behind him.

"He's sunk," AJ said.

"A goner," Tim seconded.

"Your hands are shaking, you poor slob," Matt added.

"Hey, is that drool coming out of his mouth?" AJ said.

"I don't know why I waste my time with you," Nick said. He upended his beer.

"Because we're your best friends," Tim pointed out.

"Don't depress me."

"You know you love us." Matt punched his shoulder.

AJ shook his head. "Easy, Matt. I wouldn't get too close, Nicky might be getting desperate."

"Damn right I'm desperate if you three are the best I can do for friends," Nick said. They all knew they were just mouthing off. When he'd lost his mind and embezzled the money and then it had hit the news, he'd found out who his true friends were. Most of the guys he'd known no longer gave him the time of day. But AJ, Matt and Tim had stuck with him through thick and thin.

"C'mon, Nick. You know you'll miss us next week."

"Can't say that I will. I'm looking forward to not being around." And that was more than the truth. He could use a change of scenery—even if it was only the other side of the city. It'd be better not to be around the familiar. Like when he'd quit smoking a couple of years ago and it'd been a matter of not lighting up when he was used to. A change of scenery would probably curb his wanting a woman around. And if that smacked of habit and addiction, well, these guys didn't have to know.

"How long are you gonna be gone?" Tim asked, bringing the conversation back to where it had been before Polly had brushed against Nick.

"Three days." Long past were the days when he worked around money. He'd blown that career when he'd embezzled funds. His prospects had looked dim to dismal until he'd heard about this job through a friend of a cousin's friend. Amazingly, Mack Enterprises was willing to take a chance on a guy with his history. Nick knew he was damn lucky he'd stumbled into anything better than scrubbing toilets at Fenway Park. Actually, he enjoyed his job as a booking agent for Mack Enterprises. And he was good at what he did. But for the past couple of weeks…it wasn't anything he could put his finger on…

"So, you're gonna be in Boston, but you're staying in a hotel?" Tim frowned. "Man, that doesn't make any sense."

"I'm a company man and that's where they want me so that's where I'll be."

"Seems like this trip came up pretty sudden," Matt said.

Nick shrugged. "It was a little last minute, but apparently the guy they were going to send was needed somewhere else. Me? I go where I'm needed." And he'd keep his eyes and ears open. Crazy as it sounded, the people at Mack were *too* nice, *too* trusting considering his recent history. It simply didn't feel right. But the best thing to do was to keep a low profile and his eyes and ears open. Maybe he was imagining things.

"We thought you were road tripping, so we all went together and got you a little going away present," AJ said.

They were grinning like a trio of monkeys and Nick knew major grief was about to come his way.

AJ pulled a box wrapped in plain brown paper out from beneath the table.

"It's a little something for your trip. When you're sitting in your lonely hotel room," AJ said. "Go ahead. Open it. It won't bite."

The three of them cracked up at that. Oh, boy. Nick tore off the paper. The vacuous grin of a blow-up doll stared up at him from the cardboard box.

"Meet Sheila. She's got thunder from Down

Under. We didn't want you to get too lonely," AJ said.

"Triple E's in a box," Matt said. Matt had a serious obsession with large breasts.

"Notice she's a blonde." Tim pointed out the obvious. "And she even comes with prerecorded messages, personalized just for you."

Matt snickered. "We know how important deep conversation is to you."

"If you don't like Sheila, we can return her for you. She had a sister in the box next to her," AJ said.

He looked the box over. "On no. I'll keep her. I have a feeling Sheila and I are going to get along just fine."

FIVE DAYS LATER, Nick set up his laptop on the small table in the corner of the hotel room. He put his underwear in the dresser, hung his shirts and slacks and stored his suitcase in the hotel closet. He crossed the room to the box sitting on one of the chairs next to the table.

"Okay, Sheila, my love, time for you to come out of the box." Nick opened the box, laughing. He wasn't giving AJ, Matt and Tim the upper hand with this joke. No way. He'd brought the lovely Sheila along. Now he planned to blow her up, take a digital photo of them together and e-mail it to the guys.

Sheila turned out to be five foot three and all plastic woman. Nick shook his head. He'd man-

•

aged to make it to almost thirty without firsthand knowledge of a blow-up doll. The lovely Sheila should at least put on a shirt. That's all he needed, to be arrested for Internet porn involving a blow-up doll. He pulled a button-down out of the mirrored closet, crossed the room and slid one of her arms into the shirtsleeve. He grabbed her hand to pull it through.

"Ohhh, Nicky, would you like me to talk dirty to you?" said a tinny, pseudo sexy voice with a distinct Australian accent, startling him.

He'd forgotten. The well-endowed Sheila came with personalized recorded messages. Apparently the key to conversation with Sheila was squeezing her hand.

What the heck. He might as well hear what she had to say. Nick squeezed again.

"Oh. Nicky, you're so big."

He laughed and listened to the next message.

"Nicky, big boy, I'd really like you to put your big rod inside me."

"Nicky, you make me so hot."

"Nicky, I'll do whatever you want me to do. I'm your personal love slave."

"I've been so lonely without you, Nicky. Come to Mama."

"Oh, Nicky, you're too much man for me. Maybe I should invite my hot, horny friend over, too."

"You've been a very naughty boy, Nicky. Do you need a spanking?"

Okay. Sheila's prerecorded messages offered a little something for everyone. He pulled her other arm through the shirt and smoothed it over her shoulders, encountering a switch on the back of her neck. He flipped the switch and Sheila, the Aussie lass, took off like a plastic doll possessed, vibrating wildly from the waist down, her triple-E's bobbing like water balloons in a juggling act. Laughing, Nick reached beneath the blond hair and turned her off.

Sheesh. He had to hand it to his buddies, when they bought a blow-up doll, they bought the top of the line.

And despite all of her attributes, Sheila didn't do a thing for him. It'd been so long since he'd had any kind of contact, if you discounted Polly's breasts brushing against his back, he was relieved Sheila wasn't doing a thing for him.

He set his digital camera up on the table and positioned Sheila into a seated, semireclined pose in one of the chairs. Setting the timer, he ran over and perched on her lap, one arm draped around her shoulders. The camera went off and he checked the shot. Excellent. In no time he downloaded it to his laptop, added the caption "I think I'm in love" and sent it to AJ, Tim and Matt. He grinned. Those jerks would roll on the floor.

He was in control and decided he'd head to the bar downstairs for a burger and a beer.

SERENA CHECKED HER weapon in her purse before she left the stall of the hotel bar's bathroom. That was one of the challenges of going undercover in a short skirt, thigh-high boots and a form-fitting top—it didn't leave many options to carry concealed. Now she just had to find her man.

She entered the dimly lit bar, typical for a hotel lounge. As plans went, hers was pretty loose. She'd hang out in the bar, as if she was waiting for someone and pray that no one mistook her for a hooker—only because she wouldn't be able to blow her cover by arresting any potential john that propositioned her.

She'd noticed a karaoke sign when she'd come in. If she didn't find a guy fitting Slick Nick's description, she already planned to get up and perform the old Devo song, "Whip It," in hopes of catching Mr. Paddle-Me's attention. And if that didn't work, next she'd go to Boy George's "Do You Really Want to Hurt Me?" In the past Serena's success came in having a loose plan and then punting—or improvising—as the situation unfolded. Although Captain Worth had argued with her more than once that she should always have a contingency plan, her way had worked just fine on all her other cases.

She hoped it didn't come down to karaoke because she couldn't sing, couldn't dance and she didn't look like a dominatrix. Not that she supposed there was a set formula for how a dominatrix looked, but she was fairly certain on most days she didn't fit the bill.

She knew she looked like the girl next door

with her honey-blond hair, snub nose and freckles. She looked like a girl you could trust and confide in, which was a big bonus in catching crooks, because for the most part, crooks couldn't keep their mouths shut and they always thought she was the perfect person to spill their guts to.

After nine years, it still cracked her up, the look on the criminal-du-jour's face when she whipped out her cuffs and started reciting the Miranda.

She slid onto a stool at one end of the bar, which afforded a sweeping view of the room without leaving her back exposed, and ordered a wine cooler. Lesson number one in bar crawling: Never order a drink with a wide mouth on the glass. It was too easy for a scumbag to slip in a date-rape drug. Martini glasses were the worst.

"Buy you a drink?" A guy with red hair slid onto the stool next to her. He had the look of a regular about him. She'd worked undercover long enough to recognize the signs—the casual nod to the barkeep, the ultracasual dress. And she'd found it sort of amazing that even hotel bars had a retinue of regulars, just like freaking Cheers.

"I'm covered, but thanks." She made sure she sounded friendly and nonthreatening.

"Mind a little company?"

"Not at all. I'm waiting for my friend and it can be a little intimidating sitting in a bar alone, if you know what I mean."

"Especially a pretty girl like you." Cheeser. She pasted on a smile and managed not to roll her eyes. "I'm Stephen...with a ph." His smile said he thought that was a clever line. She'd bet the farm it wasn't the first time he'd used it.

"Serena. It's nice to meet you, Stephen."

"Serena and Stephen. Bet you can't say that five times fast."

Oh, boy, he was a live one. Small wonder he was alone. "I'd better not even try it."

"You know, tonight's karaoke night."

"I saw the sign when I came in. Are you a performer?"

Stephen preened a bit. "I've been known to take the mike a time or two." He pressed his knee against hers. "I'm really good in a duet...if you're up for it...later."

Heaven forbid. She shook her head, angling for shy and modest instead of horrified. "I don't know. I've never done anything like that before."

And if luck ran her way, she wouldn't tonight. She basically sounded like a cat yowling in heat when she sang. Not pretty.

"I bet you're a fast learner and I'd love to give you a lesson or two."

"That's a generous offer, Stephen."

"Drink up and order another one. It helps take the edge off before you perform."

"I think I'd better take it slow. What kind of songs do you like to perform? I'm sure you have favorites."

Typical man. Ask him a question about himself and he was off and running. She just had to look interested and interject the occasional *"hmmm," "really"* or *"oh, that's interesting,"* and he'd drone on endlessly about his karaoke prowess.

Stephen was in the middle of a performance recount, when Slick Nick arrived. Serena spotted him the moment he walked into the bar. Six feet and a few inches, black hair, cut short and brushed back—a good cut, an expensive cut, not the twelve-buck, walk-in-off-the-street cut that she splurged on for herself. Nice clothes. Thirtyish. Obviously in good shape. He carried himself like a man comfortable in his own skin, assured, as if he was used to people looking at him.

A slight shiver of some second-sense recognition whispered through her. She recognized his face. Knew she'd seen him before. That grainy photo was better than she'd thought because his face definitely registered with her. This was her man. She felt it bone deep and the flush that spread through her wasn't attraction. It couldn't possibly be. She was merely excited she'd finally found Slick Nick.

She remained calm and zeroed back in on Stephen-with-a-ph who was generously sharing his tips on audience control when you had the mike.

Stephen's pager buzzed. He checked it and made a face. "It's my mother. I've got to run her over to bingo at the VFW." He stood up. "But I'll be back in time for the karaoke." He snapped and pointed his finger at her. "Don't sing that duet without me."

The dark-haired man pulled out a chair a couple of tables away from the bar.

Serena bit back the observation that if she was singing without him, it wouldn't be a duet. "I promise—no duets without you." And she no longer had to worry about how to get rid of Stephen. Thank you, Mom and bingo at the VFW.

Stephen left and she sat alone at the bar. Heat tingled over her skin. She looked up. The dark-haired man was watching her. She held his gaze with her own. Something ancient passed between them, a recognition, an acknowledgement, an attraction that sent a tremor through her. She looked away first, thoroughly disconcerted by the potency of just that glance.

She busied herself sipping her wine cooler and reconnected with her equilibrium. Serena checked him out from beneath her lashes. Her fishnets and thigh-high black boots had definitely snagged his interest. She smiled and crossed her legs.

His answering smile, a slow sensual acknowledgement, set off a flutter low in her belly that had nothing to do with being a cop and everything to do with being a woman. Easy there, girlfriend. He was a criminal and a pervert, and all of that aside, he had a little thingie—and God knows two of the three guys she'd dated in the past ten years had fallen into the little thingie category.

He deliberately looked away from her, as if he'd caught himself staring. That was okay—he'd definitely noticed her and had liked what he'd seen. It was about time this case started going somewhere.

The waitress approached his table and Serena took advantage of his distraction to assess him, strictly for ID purposes, of course. Hair with just a hint of curl that said it would riot out of control if he skipped a trim or two. His shirt hugged broad shoulders. She'd guess somewhere between one-eighty and one-ninety-five pounds. Muscle weighed more than fat and he was definitely carrying lean muscle on that body. From where she sat, no moles, scars, tattoos—of course, she was sure he was sitting on the tattoo—or other distinguishing marks were visible except when he turned his head to look at the waitress. It looked as if his ear had been pierced, but he didn't wear an earring now. It didn't take a leap of imagination to envision him with a small gold hoop in his ear. There was something sexy and roguish about him. She'd seen a sleepy sensuality in his eyes when they'd locked with hers.

What was she thinking? Well, that was, in fact, the problem. She wasn't thinking. There was nothing cerebral about his effect on her. Her heart raced. With one look, he'd managed to heat up some of her body parts long neglected.

He ordered a beer and a medium-rare burger, hold the onion. When the waitress tried to flirt with him, he shut her down with a tense smile. It certainly wasn't the sensual zinger he'd sent Serena's way. His cell phone chirped and he flipped it open and up to his ear. "Nick, here."

She sipped her wine cooler to hide her triumphant smile and leaned forward slightly, the better to eavesdrop on his conversation.

"Yeah. They sent me because bookings have been down a bit and you know I'm always willing to help a fool part with his money. Okay, yeah, that really wasn't funny. I know, Rourke. Prison's not something to joke about. Okay, that was in bad taste. I know I'm lucky."

She had hit the mother lode. This had to be Slick Nick. Your average Joe off the street didn't consider prison an option. Could life get any sweeter?

"Yeah. Catch you later. By the way, I'm staying at The Barrister, room 583, if you need me and can't get me on my cell."

That answered that question. Life could get sweeter and it just had. If she was into astrology, she'd think her stars or planets or whatever they were had just aligned. Now, she just needed to stall him in the bar while she checked out room 583.

"HERE'S YOUR BEER. Should I bring another one when I bring your burger?" the waitress asked, putting his drink on the table in front of him.

"No thanks. I'm good."

He looked past the waitress, avoiding the eye contact she sought. That was a big mistake because it left him looking at the leggy blonde sitting at the bar. He'd been so good when he came in the room. He'd made sure he didn't look around the room. Better not to even know what he was missing out on.

And then he'd seen *her* at the bar and his whole world had shifted, tilted, come into focus. It was as if every cliché of meeting a stranger's eyes across a crowded room had blossomed inside him at that moment in time. For the span of several heartbeats the people and all the noise of the bar had faded to nothingness and it had only been him and her.

Damn it to hell. Twenty-eight days and none of the women AJ and Matt had thrown at him had interested him, certainly none had tempted him.

And now, he saw this woman. She definitely tempted him. She wasn't particularly beautiful but she was pretty in a fresh-scrubbed way and those legs in those boots… His sex drive had returned from its twenty-eight day hiatus with a vengeance.

Damn. The smart thing would've been to order room service and eat in with Sheila. He almost told the waitress to box it up to go and then he stopped himself. He was made of sterner stuff than that.

Nope. He was not going to think about running his hand over the smooth curve of her calf and along the delicate line of her ankle. No sir. Not even going to imagine those legs wrapped around him. Nuh-uh.

He glanced up from those incredible legs and

found her watching him with faint amusement. A little thrill coursed through him until his brain cells caught up with his hormones. He deliberately looked away. He'd concentrate on his beer. Two days. He had two lousy, long days to go. He could he do it. He would do it.

He definitely didn't need to look into those eyes or ogle those legs again. Why torture himself when he couldn't even introduce himself? What would he say? "Hey, I'd like to get to know you a little better. Mind if I call you in three days when this bet is off with my friends?" She'd think he and his friends possessed the mentality and maturity of adolescent schoolboys. While that might well be the case, he didn't need to advertise it.

The waitress delivered his burger and a bottle of catsup. "Can I get you anything else?"

Nick demurred and forced himself not to look at the blonde at the bar. So, they'd exchanged a look and a smile. Big deal. He bit into his burger and concentrated on savoring the flavor of ground sirloin, a toasted Kaiser bun, fresh lettuce, a ripe juicy tomato and a thick slice of pungently sharp cheddar cheese. But he was still conscious, in his peripheral vision, of those shapely legs shifting.

Nick was two bites into his burger when he saw the woman stand in his peripheral vision. No. Please don't let her stop by his table. He was in a weakened state. She walked past and, idiotically, he found himself disappointed. But there was nothing wrong with his sense of smell and she smelled as good as she looked. A light and airy scent with an underlying tone of seduction. Hell, who was he kidding? At this point the damned hamburger smelled seductive.

He watched her walk, mesmerized by the length of her legs, the sway of her hips in that short skirt. And those black, thigh-hugging, stiletto-heeled boots made him ache. She was obviously a woman who worked out. She looked toned and lean. Nick forgot he had a mouthful of ground beef and swallowed, promptly choking.

Dangerously close to needing the Heimlich maneuver, with his eyes watering, he missed where she went. That was just as well, since she was none of his business.

He concentrated on his burger and the ball game playing silently on the bar TV. He was relieved the blonde with the boots had left. Really, he was. He wasn't in the least disappointed. So, she'd started his engine in a major way just by walking by. It was his lucky day that she'd left. He'd take his time, have a nice leisurely meal and watch the game. He could relax now that temptation had left the building.

He winced as Bastion, a new closer for the Sox, allowed a grand slam. Another Sox game down the toilet. The waitress arrived with another beer.

"I didn't order that," Nick said.

"Compliments of the lady at the bar." The waitress, who didn't look old enough to drink beer, much less serve it, winked at him.

"What lady?"

She pointed to where the blonde had been. "She was over there. She said to send this over and she'd be back in a few minutes."

Nick made a strangled noise. "I need my check."

"Was something wrong with your burger?"

"No. Yeah. Maybe. I just need to leave."

The waitress gave him a look that said he was cute but seriously psycho. Let her think he was psycho. He didn't care. All he knew was that he didn't plan to wait around for Ms. Legs to return. His willpower was already stretched thin. In fact, he was fresh out. He needed to get the hell out of Dodge before those legs and that cute freckled nose showed up at his table.

Forget the rest of his burger. He upended the beer—a fresh beer was a terrible thing to waste. His best course of action was to put as much distance between him and that long-legged, sweet-smelling siren. He couldn't get back to his room fast enough.

3

SERENA EASED the hotel room door closed behind her. She turned and saw a woman sitting in the chair across the room and nearly jumped out of her skin. Adrenaline surged through her. Was the woman dead or tied up? Serena realized she was neither, because she wasn't a woman, she was a freaking blow-up doll wearing a man's shirt. What the heck?

She shook her head and crossed the room, eager to have a look at the laptop open on the round table. Her luck had definitely taken a turn today. Who knew? Maybe she'd find all the incriminating evidence she needed at once.

What she saw on the screen was incriminating all right. Slick Nick perched on the doll's lap, nuzzling her neck. And the sicko had even posted a caption across the bottom. "I think I'm in love." Ick. With a plastic doll.

Just went to prove you should never, ever judge a book by its cover. Slick Nick looked like a regular, sexy, hot guy. He looked *nice*. Certainly not like you'd expect him to cozy up with a blow-up doll and get off on a little spanking. This guy's kink factor was way off her meter.

She rifled through the folders in his briefcase, taking care to leave everything the way she'd found it. Nothing definitive there, except the name Nick O'Malley, plus a phone number and address. They knew Slick Nick used a number of aliases. O'Malley was close enough to Malone to make sense as an alias. People tended to pick names similar to their own. But the address… She grinned. Sweet.

She stepped back and turned around, bumping the chair behind her. The doll started to fall and Serena grabbed it to keep it from tumbling to the floor.

"Oh, Nicky, would you like me to talk dirty to you?" a canned woman's voice asked, startling Serena. Serena realized it was the doll. This guy was a bonafide freak. Serena righted the doll, feeling slightly intimidated in the face of what were extremely large breasts. Apparently Slick Nick did not find more than a mouthful a waste. Those monsters would require a quarterback to make a two-handed pass. Wait till the boys in the station heard about this.

And then because she figured Nick hadn't even finished his burger yet and it was sort of akin to watching a train wreck or *Jerry Springer* when you were late-night channel surfing, she squeezed the doll again.

"Oh, Nicky, you're so big."

Oh brother. This guy was pa-thet-ic. And then, because she wasn't sure that it wouldn't come in handy one day and because she was simply curious, she listened to the rest of the doll's messages. Sheesh. Love slave. Mama. Threesome. Spanking. Well, Slick Nick certainly had some hot buttons.

She did a quick recon of the drawers. Not much there except for the usual socks, underwear—kind of boring tighty whities, not exactly what she'd figured for a kinky kind of guy—and a pair of cotton drawstring pants all jumbled together. Nick might be a nice dresser but he wasn't exactly tidy or organized.

She only had one more place to check. Maybe he had something in the closet, something in his suitcase. She slid open the mirrored closet door and checked the pants pockets. Nada. The door lock clicked. She froze for a second, then she ducked into the closet, sliding the closet door behind her just as the room door swung open. Her heart pounded. Two seconds later and she'd have been an unwilling doorstop.

The deadbolt clicked into place, a sure sign that whoever had come in—she assumed Nick— didn't plan on going back out any time soon. She was amazed she could hear anything over the deafening pounding of her heart. That had been a close call. Nick walked past the closet and Serena held her breath, careful to remain still and not bump the hangers at shoulder level. Thank goodness he'd left half the closet empty. She inched the closet door open, just a hair, so that she could survey the room.

Slick Nick sat at the table next to the blow-up doll and did something on the computer. "Ah, sweet Sheila, you're still here." Double ick. His plastic fantasy had a name. And where the heck else did he expect her to be? Sheila wasn't going far on rubber legs. "I should've ordered in and eaten with you, my sweet."

It was one of those universal injustices that such a weirdo had such a sexy voice, a warm, slightly husky baritone that slid over you, through you.

"There was a woman in the bar…my God, those legs. I was seriously tempted."

He was talking about her. She wasn't sure whether she was flattered or grossed out. Well, that wasn't true. Maybe all his perversion was rubbing off, because, dammit, she was flattered that he was out there sighing over her legs and confessing to the plastic Sheila.

"They were get-your-dick-hard legs. Oh, honey. And those eyes and that cute nose. Sheila, she was a turn-on and I was close to caving, but I stayed the course, even if it meant leaving half my dinner. I didn't give in to temptation. I was true to you, my love." He closed his eyes and ran a hand over his head. "I swear I can even smell her perfume in here. She seriously flipped my switch." He opened his eyes and shook his head, as if to clear it.

Serena couldn't believe that it turned her on to hear Mr. Perve talk about getting a woody looking at her legs, especially since he was describing her to his blow-up doll girlfriend. She didn't want to feel the moisture gather between her thighs, didn't want to feel that flutter low in her belly. It was even worse when she considered that his "giving in to temptation" meant betraying an inanimate object with a permanently gaping mouth.

Oh no. No flaming way. Not going to do it. No way she was going to sit in this closet and watch him "enjoy" Sheila. But hey, Sheila was there, available, permanently willing and he was turned on. Of course that was what was going to happen.

Cripes, a guy with a little willie going at it with a blow-up doll. Well, it wouldn't be any better if it was a guy with a big willie.

The upside, however, to witnessing that freak show in action would be she'd see his bare butt and have a positive ID. Sometimes her job sucked. Increasingly, she felt permanently slimed by the bad guys.

"Okay, little Sheila, I think it's time you went in the closet."

What?

Nick picked up the doll and carried her under one arm across the room.

No. No. No. A blow-up doll was about to totally blow her cover. She inched back but couldn't go too far because his suitcase was on the foldout stand and his clothes were hanging. If she was really lucky, he'd only open the door far enough to shove the doll in. But she wasn't feeling lucky about right now.

Nick reached for the closet slide and must've hit Sheila's hand. "Oh, Nicky, would you like me to talk dirty to you?"

"Thanks for the offer, Sheila, but I don't think so." He laughed but turned back toward the bed, away from the closet. "But I guess you can just stay in the chair. You're really too nice a girl to be stuck in the closet."

Reprieved! Blood rushed to Serena's head.

"Enjoy your chair while I shower." He placed the doll in the chair and crossed to the dresser where he pulled out the cotton drawstring pants.

Shower meant naked. Bare tush. All she needed was one good look, just a glimpse of that tattoo. No. She was not looking forward to checking out his bod. She was just doing her job—even if that meant watching a buff, good-looking perve strip naked.

Serena wasn't sure how much longer she could hold this position, scrunched over. Nick went into the bathroom. *Don't close the door.* He pushed it behind him, but it only closed about a quarter of the way, leaving her with a line of sight and the reflection from the bathroom mirror.

He tossed the cotton pants onto the counter next to the sink and reached into the shower, turning on the water. Serena took advantage of the moment to kneel on the closet floor, closer to the crack, giving her a better view without her eye being level with his in the mirror. She didn't need him to see her watching him from the closet. That could be a bad scene. But from what she knew of this guy, he'd probably get off on it.

Nick tugged his shirt over his head and tossed it onto the floor, taking her right back to that life-not-fair deal. He had a gorgeous chest, broad with a smattering of hair that was masculine without looking like a hairy beast. And the mirror reflected his back—no hair, thank you, but plenty of sculpted muscle. And arms—cut, defined. He was buff without being Cro-Magnon.

He stepped out of a pair of loafers and unzipped his pants, sliding them down well-muscled legs. Now who was the freaking pervert? She was crouched in a closet watching a man undress. She felt as if she should close her eyes or look away, but that would defeat the purpose of getting a look at his butt and that was, after all, why she was here. She kept her eyes trained on the nearly naked, very fine male specimen before her.

Nick hooked his thumbs in his underwear and pulled them off, stepping back slightly, so that his butt was just behind the door. Serena gaped. Sweet mother of…oh my. He had a magic wand waving that looked pretty big from where she crouched. He pivoted on his right foot and turned toward the door, giving her a bird's eye, full-frontal nudity view. She bit back the sound that almost escaped her. Case in point, one woman's stallion was another woman's foal, because there was nada wrong with the equipment he was packing up front. If his ex-girlfriend wanted to see little… well, Serena should introduce the woman to Serena's last two boyfriends. Nick here made them look like they needed to shop in the boy's department. Wow. He flipped the switch for the fan and then pivoted back around. Blocked by the door, he got in the shower.

Damn. She ought to smack herself. She'd been so busy ogling his package, she'd missed the perfect opportunity to check out his rear which would've been reflected in the mirror. Now, when she would have had the chance to slip out the door while he was in the shower, she had to wait around in the closet, hoping she'd catch a glimpse of it when he stepped out.

There was no use beating herself up about it. That had definitely been a distraction. She was pretty sure there wasn't a woman alive who wouldn't have found herself…interested in that view.

She might as well try to stretch a bit and switch positions while he had the shower going, although she didn't dare risk sliding the closet door open. She carefully moved the empty hangers to the other end so she wouldn't bump against them. God knows how long she was going to be stuck in here. She hoped he wasn't a night owl. She sat on the closet floor, yoga style.

The scent of his cologne clung faintly to his

clothes. Tempting. Tantalizing. Even his clothes smelled sexy. He looked good—make that great. He smelled good. He even sounded good. What a shame he was a bad guy. And what the heck was wrong with her? All she'd ever felt on any other case had been a sense of detachment and loathing for the perp. Hard as she tried, she couldn't find that detachment now. Nick Malone, aka, Nick O'Malley, was fully deserving of her loathing. Unfortunately, she couldn't muster it. Somehow he had slipped in under her radar. Something about him had felt intensely personal, intimate, from the time she'd met his eyes across the room, to when she'd listened to him talk to a blow-up doll about how Serena affected him, until now when she sat surrounded by his scent. Something about this man pierced the protective armor she'd always instinctively cloaked herself in and touched her, engaged her. She felt betrayed by her reaction, her attraction to him, but it was something she couldn't seem to quell and she couldn't deny. And in that moment she learned something important about herself and choices and mankind in general. This man was reprehensible, and against all rationale and against everything she stood for and believed in, she felt a connection, a pull to him that was totally out of her control. She could despise herself, she could berate herself, but it didn't seem to change her instinctive response to Nick Malone. What she could control, however, was what actions she took. She'd make a positive ID and then she'd turn the case over to Worth and he could reassign it. Any of the boys should be glad to take on a case that was almost in the bag.

A sound from the shower interrupted her train of thought. There it was again. Was it a moan? Maybe she'd imagined that deep, throaty sound. She heard it again. It wasn't her imagination. She wasn't exactly naive, but it took a moment for her to figure it out, a few seconds before she recognized the noise of a man aroused. God. She was sitting in a closet alone and she still blushed—she could feel the heat wash over her. Obviously his hand and his imagination were both being used on that impressive erection she'd seen not too long ago.

She wet her suddenly dry lips. She'd done that. She'd heard his confession to his plastic girlfriend. The intensity and frequency of his moans increased and another type of heat fired through her. Just as she'd been helpless against the attraction she'd felt earlier, she couldn't seem to suppress her reaction to him masturbating in the shower. She bit down on her lower lip but still her nipples tightened and her thighs grew wet in response to what she overheard. Please. She really couldn't take much more of this. She was embarrassed and frustrated, and dammit, suddenly and incredibly turned on. It was uncanny, almost as if he shared some cosmic wavelength with her, but he came then in one long moaning release.

The water stopped. She knelt again, making sure her body wasn't visible through the crack, and peeked out. He reached for a towel, his dark, hair-covered arm dripping water. Steam rendered the mirror useless. She couldn't see him while he toweled off—he was too far into the room. He stepped forward, picked up the loose cotton pants and stepped into them. Talk about frustrating. Between the door angle and a streak of bad luck, she couldn't see his butt.

While he brushed his teeth, she stared at what was a very nice butt, peering hard, hoping for a glimpse of a tattoo. If his pants had been white, or off-white, or muslin, the tattoo might have shown through, but it was a lost cause with a dark plaid print. Even though it was pointless, she watched him floss, put on deodorant and run his hand through his wet hair. Of course, it wasn't as if she had much else to do or look at, stuck in the closet.

He grabbed another clean towel, turned off the bathroom light and the vent fan, and walked out of the bathroom, his dirty clothes still heaped on the floor. He was a slob and a pervert, but he was clean. And breath-stealingly sexy. Her breath caught in her throat. When he passed the closet, she smelled the intoxicating mixture of soap, warm skin and deodorant.

From her vantage point, she could only see about half of the bed. Nick spread the towel on the floor at the bottom corner. Oh no, now Sheila was about to get it. This guy was insatiable. Wasn't once in the shower enough for him? Apparently not.

And at this point she wasn't so sure she knew herself any longer. Once upon a time, she would've known with certainty that watching a guy with a blow-up doll would disgust her. But once upon a time, she also would've bet the farm she wouldn't hide in a closet while a guy got off in the shower. She would not, however, watch him engage in sex with a blow-up doll—once she got a look at his tush. She'd study the edge of frayed carpet butting up to the metal track of the sliding closet door.

Nick stretched out on the towel and propped his feet up on the edge of the bed. Serena almost laughed out loud. Sit-ups. The guy was powering through flaming sit-ups. Which explained that body—the nice flat belly with its six-pack of rippling muscle. After about a minute, she started counting. He just kept going and going, the muscles in his shoulders and his back a fine sight to watch. Hey, she was stuck here, she might as well make the most of it.

Nick stood, picked up the towel and tossed it onto the other chair. His cell phone rang. Serena held her breath, hoping it was a call about his impending meeting.

"Hi, Ma…. No, you're not bothering me. I'm just getting ready to go to bed. How's Da feeling?… Yeah, make sure he takes his medicine. We need him well for his surprise birthday party, don't we?…Yep. I mentioned it to the boys and they can all come… Right. Sure, Ma, I'll take my vitamins… Love you too. Talk to you later. 'Night."

He sounded like such a nice person. A good son, loving, concerned, dutiful. Did his mother have a clue what her son really did? She doubted it, if the woman was reminding her thirty-year-old son to take his vitamins. She hardened her heart. It was tough when you thought about the innocent people criminals hurt with their lifestyle, all the parents, spouses and children that lived with the consequences of those actions. Did his mother know about his tush tattoo? Did she know about his little spanking fetish?

Nick turned down the cover on the king-size bed and grabbed the remote. He flipped the TV to a sports channel. She heard him sign off the laptop and close it. He stretched out on the bed, folding his hands beneath his head.

Serena settled on the closet floor.

She was so screwed.

A HAZE OF CIGARETTE SMOKE hung in the air and a cold sweat trickled down Nick Malone's back. Jo-Jo was not going to be pleased and Nick was about to get a taste of that displeasure. Big Al, looking every inch the thug he was in a suit that didn't quite fit his bulging biceps and thick bull neck, walked over. "Jo-Jo'll see you now."

Big Al shadowed him to the door where another

equally massive guard, Marcel, stood. Nick reached for the doorknob. Big Al wrapped a meaty hand around his arm. "Leave the piece with Marcel. You'll get it back when you're done."

Nick pulled the 357 from the shoulder holster beneath his suit jacket and handed it to Marcel. Big Al still held on to his arm. "And don't forget about the one on your ankle."

It'd been worth a try. He lied through his teeth. "I hadn't got that far yet."

"Just hand it over."

Big Al had the stereotypical thug build, but what made him even more intimidating was that he wasn't your typical garden-variety big, dumb guy. Big Al was cunning and ruthless *and* big—an intimidating combination. No one saw Jo-Jo without going through Big Al and no one went through Big Al if he didn't want them to. Big Al reminded Nick of a crocodile he'd seen once at the reptile house. It owned the same cold, unblinking stare.

Nick fished the double-shot derringer out of the ankle holster and straightened his pant cuffs. He might be in trouble, but he wouldn't go in with his pant leg stuck in his sock. He'd go in with panache.

Big Al released his arm. "Don't keep the boss waiting."

Nick paused and deliberately brushed his suit jacket arm where Big Al's hand had just been and then he opened Jo-Jo's office door. He didn't have to worry about closing it behind him. Two more beefy guys flanked the door inside. Nick's legs shook as he crossed the room. Big Al was dangerous but he didn't frighten Nick. Neither did the two goons behind him. Jo-Jo, however, scared the hell out of him.

Silence, fraught with disapproval, shrouded the room like a heavy velvet curtain. The carpet's thick, plush pile absorbed his footsteps as he crossed the room. Nick settled into a club chair in front of the ornately carved desk. His uncle's tall chair, upholstered in the finest leather, was turned, its back facing him. Jo-Jo appreciated the finer things in life.

Even as a young boy, that had been something he'd had in common with his uncle Jo-Jo. It had pained Jo-Jo to witness the dismal living conditions his nephew Nick and his sister Angelina had endured as Nick's father—a good, kind man, but inept—had failed at one endeavor after another, shackling them in poverty. Nick had been fourteen, a boy transitioning into manhood, when his father had met with an "unfortunate accident," one Jo-Jo had manufactured. Nick's beautiful, fragile mother had been devastated by the loss of her husband. Nick had never recounted the chilling conversation he'd overheard that had left no doubt about who had been behind his father's death. Nick thought it would totally destroy his mother to know the brother she adored had disposed of her beloved husband like offending offal.

And Nick had enough street smarts that he'd made sure Jo-Jo never found out just how much he, Nick, knew. But, at fourteen, he learned a quick, harsh lesson about where kindness and good intentions got a man versus cunning and power. He saw who was alive and who was dead.

With his dad out of the picture, Jo-Jo had stepped in as Nick's father figure. He'd pulled them out of the rat-infested, graffiti-covered neighborhood. Jo-Jo had brought death and destruction to his family, but conversely had plucked them out of poverty and given Nick access to the finer things in life and given him opportunity. Nick regarded Jo-Jo with a mix of fear, loathing, admiration and respect. In Nick's world, his uncle was pretty damn near God. Jo-Jo giveth and Jo-Jo taketh away.

The chair swiveled slowly, bringing Nick face-to-face with his uncle.

Jo-Jo leaned forward and put a Game Boy on his desk. He leaned back in his chair and smiled at Nick. Nick's gut tightened. As usual, Jo-Jo looked affable and mild, the personification of a vague, favorite uncle. And as usual, his smile never quite reached his eyes. Nick always found Jo-Jo's smile chilling.

"I'm disappointed, Nicky. I get a call from a mutual friend and you know what he says to me?" Nick kept his mouth shut. It was a rhetorical question. "He tells me, 'Your nephew could fuck up a wet dream.'" Of course, that cop wasn't original enough to come up with something new. He kept recycling the same insult. "Do you know how that makes me feel, Nicky? It doesn't make me feel good. All my careful planning, months of setting this up. I see a man in the paper who has committed a crime and yet he hasn't gone to jail. And I ask myself who would hire such a man now? Who would give him a decent job? Who would trust him? I think he would be grateful for a good job. And I also think he looks like you, same build, same height, close in age. And my wheels are turning, because I'm a very smart man. I work it so that he gets hired by my company. I have all the pieces in place. I hand you opportunity on a platter and you repay my genius with carelessness. Without our mutual friend, you would be enjoying the comfort of a very small jail cell right now. How can you respect me and be so careless?"

Jo-Jo folded his hands across his stomach, a signal that Nick better have something to say for himself. Nick's pits poured sweat. This was like crossing an open field littered with land mines. "I have the utmost respect for you and your genius, Jo-Jo. I'm horrified I was so careless. I know I compromised your plans, but I think I've repaired any damage. I changed my meeting location and arranged for O'Malley to go to the original place. In a way, this works out better."

"Except the police will know Nick O'Malley isn't you when they don't find a tattoo."

"I've thought of that and I'll get rid of mine and

then neither of us will have one. I'm having it removed." It was going to be expensive and he was essentially destroying a piece of art, but he'd heard it hurt like hell. He was looking forward to that part.

"How much of it is gone?"

"None so far."

"Get on it. Now."

"Yes, Jo-Jo."

"What are you waiting for? I told you to get on it now."

Nick stood. "I'll go right now." He crossed the room.

Jo-Jo halted him at the door.

"Nick, these other things he tells me about you…they sicken me. Now get out of my sight."

Nick nodded and left. The other things…there had been no need for Jo-Jo to be told. When his usefulness was over, which was when O'Malley took the fall, that cop was a dead man walking.

4

FINALLY. SERENA EASED UP from her position on the closet floor, her cramped muscles screaming in protest. She'd thought he'd never go to sleep. How much sports could a man possibly watch? And while she'd heard enough baseball and ESPN to last her a lifetime, she supposed she should be grateful he hadn't tuned into some raunchy pay-per-view sex channel and pulled his blow-up honey into bed with him.

She slid open the closet door. It hadn't really been that long. An hour and a half passed much slower when you were stuffed in a closet and even slower when you were still sort of hot and bothered and tingling in places you had no business tingling in while on a stakeout and feeling all the guiltier for it. And she was starving. At least the guys on surveillance got coffee and donuts. She'd just about kill for a corned beef on rye from McCaffrey's Diner or even a freaking jelly donut and cup of coffee.

Serena silently drew a deep breath and slowly, quietly exhaled. She'd been stuck in the closet, surrounded by the enticing scent of the criminal-with-the-spanking-fetish, which was how she'd thought of him while in there. It was how she *had* to think of him. She absolutely couldn't slot him as the first hot hunk who'd really, thoroughly turned her on in a long time. And he'd definitely done that.

She glanced toward the bed. The television's glow illuminated him, sprawled on his belly, one arm over his head, one knee angled to the side. You'd think he might not come across as sexy in his sleep, like maybe he'd snore loudly or drool or something. Not the case. He was as hot unconscious as he was upright and moving. Simply standing here looking at him left her heart pounding and her mouth dry. The sooner she wrapped this up, the better. She'd never ogled or been attracted to a perp before and this was a terrible time to start. Actually, there was no good time to start something so foolish.

If she had any inkling he was a heavy sleeper, she'd ease across the room and sneak a peek down the back of his sleep pants. The boob tube provided plenty of light, at least enough to spot a heart-shaped tattoo. But she had no idea how soundly Slick Nick slept and she'd have a heck of a time explaining peering down his pants if she woke him, so she'd call it a night and move on to Plan B tomorrow.

He was attracted to her—she'd seen and heard that proof first hand—so that left the door wide-open. Maybe she'd "bump into him" at breakfast in the morning. If not, she'd find another way to put herself in his path. One way or another, she would look at his bare butt and positively ID this guy. After that, it was simply a matter of time before someone in the department got the goods on him and nailed him. Then he'd share a jail cell with a guy named Bruno who'd eagerly admire his tattoo and spank him.

The idea was far more disquieting than it should be. Prison wasn't pretty—especially for a looker like Malone. But if he did the crime, he should do the time. His game came with consequences.

Serena used the edge of her shirt and eased the hotel room door handle down. A loud click echoed. Dammit. The deadbolt. She should've manually unlocked it before she turned the handle. But the TV was still on…

Light flooded the room behind her.

"You," he said, identifying her.

So much for dashing out the door unrecognized. She pivoted to face him, unsure exactly how to play this out. Brazen and deliberate usually worked best in a situation such as this. "Surprise."

He clicked off the TV, not looking surprised in the least. Amusement and a hint of exasperation sparkled in his eyes, which was weird considering he'd caught her sneaking around his room. He should've been flabbergasted. Instead he looked as if he'd almost expected her.

He got out of bed, his pants hanging distractingly low on his hips. Her pulse shifted into overdrive. "I knew AJ'd pull a stunt like this." He rubbed the back of his neck, offering a mind-riveting view of rippling arm and chest muscles and silky dark underarm hair. He slanted her a look from brilliant blue eyes fringed with thick dark lashes that probably wrecked women's blood pressure on a regular basis. "Knocking would've been safer than sneaking in."

Whew. He assumed she was coming, not going. And it sounded as if he blamed AJ, whoever that was, for her presence. She shifted her handbag on her shoulder. "Would you have let me in if I'd knocked?"

Her breath caught somewhere midchest at the heat in his eyes as he looked at her from the top of her head to the tip of her toes and all the areas in between. He crossed his arms over his chest. "No. If I had an ounce of sense, I wouldn't have let you in."

And he was probably one breath away from telling her to get the hell out. She didn't give him the opportunity. She crossed the room and perched on the edge of the bed.

"Make yourself at home. Are you comfy?"

Serena ignored his sarcasm, but not the way he eyed her legs. She leaned back, bracing her hands on the bed. His body heat lingered on the sheet beneath her palm, sending a wave of her own heat crashing through her. She crossed her legs, offering him a peek at the garters holding her stockings in place. She wet her lips with the tip of her tongue. "Thanks for asking. I'm comfy now."

Awareness filled the air between them. She knew the instant he spotted her garters. His jaw clench and intense heat flashed in his eyes. "AJ sent you, didn't he?"

She sent a silent thanks to AJ, whoever the heck he was, for unwittingly providing her with a cover. "What makes you think that?"

He laughed and aimed for nonchalance, but the muscles in his shoulders belied his tension. "You buy me a beer and then you show up in my room? Come on, I know he likes to win and I was expecting something. I should've picked up on it in the bar." As if he couldn't help himself, he dropped his eyes to the garters edging out from beneath her skirt hem. "Not something quite this bold, but…"

She had no freaking clue what he was talking about, but she'd do her part to go along. "Are you upset?"

"No." He looked away from her legs. "But AJ's underestimated me. Are you a hooker?"

She laughed, not offended in the least. She looked like a hooker and he didn't even know the half of it… yet. "No. I'm not a prostitute." She needed to shift his attention away from her and exactly how she came to be here and exactly what she was supposed to do now that she was here. She nodded toward Sheila as if she'd just spotted her. "I didn't realize you already had company."

Nick laughed and shrugged, a faint flush rising beneath the dark stubble shadowing his jaw. "AJ sent her as well."

"AJ takes care of you, doesn't he?"

"AJ likes to win."

Her cover was safe until Nick talked to the mysterious AJ. And the only sure way to keep Nick Malone, also known as Nick O'Malley, from reaching for his phone was to distract him, keep him off balance…and get his pants off. She shifted on the bed, inching her skirt further up her thighs. "I forgot to introduce myself. I'm Serena Barton."

"Nick O'Malley, but you knew that. What you also need to know is you're wasting your time here, Serena. I'm not going to sleep with you. I'm not going to kiss you. I'm not even going to touch you. You can report back to AJ that you came, you saw and you didn't conquer."

It was time for her to shift into her dominatrix persona.

She reached out and ran her hand over his leg. "That's fine."

He jumped back, out of reach. "I just told you I'm not sleeping with you."

She stood and stepped closer, trapping him between the TV cabinet and her. Before he knew what she was up to, she skimmed her hands down his lightly furred chest and over the tight muscles of his belly. Oh. He might be a bad guy but he felt yummy and her pulse raced. "Got it. No sex. No kissing. And you're not going to touch me." She slipped her index fingers into the edge of his pants, feeling a rush at the warm satin of his skin against the backs of her fingers. And if his scent had been arousing in the closet, up close and personal, it was maddening. "But we can still play." She didn't have to work at imbuing her voice with a low huskiness.

He grabbed her wrists and set her away from him, his fingers branding her bare flesh. "It's time for you to leave, Serena Barton. Thanks for stopping by." He turned her in the direction of the door.

Much as she wanted to run screaming from the room and leave behind the fire that his brief touch had ignited, she had a job to do. She executed a one-eighty and faced him again, forcing him to stop or run into close, intimate contact with her. She shook her head and scraped her fingernail down his chest. "But I just got here. We haven't had any fun yet."

He swallowed hard. Oh, yeah, she was getting to him. And the situation was getting to her more than a little bit. There was a definite current of attraction running hard and fast between them. He shook his head. "I'm not any fun. No fun at all. Nope. And I think you being here is trouble." He sounded panicked and aroused. God knows, touching him had her sizzling inside.

According to what she'd read about the domination game, he was really just begging for her to take it to the next step.

"That's not what I've heard. I've heard you're lots of fun." She reached for him and he feinted left, putting the bed between them. She made a pouty face. "Now you've hurt my feelings. Hurting my feelings was a bad idea. You've left me no choice but to take action."

She worked free the top button on her shirt. She was playing a role, but it was nearly impossible not to feel sexy when he looked at her like that.

He swallowed convulsively. "What are you doing?"

Two more and two to go. "I'm getting comfortable."

"Comfortable's a bad idea. A very bad idea." His mouth said one thing. The growing bulge in his pajama bottom told another story.

She pulled off her shirt to reveal the black leather bustier beneath. He made a strangled sound, which was very gratifying. She wasn't exactly flat but busty was a descriptive stretch as well. But she'd bought what must be the Wonderbra of the dominatrix clothing line. It turned her average breasts into…well, pretty darn impressive and the metal nipple covers were a nice authoritative touch, she'd thought. Right now her nipples were tight little buds against those metal covers.

"You need to put your shirt back on."

Probably not a bad idea before she spontaneously combusted from the heat in his eyes. But the objective was to get his pants off.

"But I'm really hot. I'm just cooling down." She slid her skirt off and his mouth dropped open when he saw the black leather micro-mini she wore beneath it with garters fully exposed. She'd thought it was hot when she saw it at the store and when she'd gotten dressed earlier today…there was no denying it was ultrasexy. Part of maintaining a good cover was getting your head into it and becoming who you were pretending to be, and right now that wasn't a problem. She felt sexy and powerful.

"No…I…bad…"

It was something of a power trip to arrest a guy, but it was also gratifying to reduce a man to almost incoherent.

She surprised herself when she climbed up onto the bed on her hands and knees. "Are you telling me you've been bad, Nick?"

Whoa. She wasn't quite sure where it had come from but she was taking to this dominatrix role like a house on fire.

"No." He choked out the single word.

"Naughty, naughty Nick," she said and crawled across the mattress. Nick stood on the other side, transfixed. "I know just what you need."

"No. I don't think you do. What I need is for you to get off of that bed and leave. Now."

She eyed his pajama bottoms that barely concealed a raging erection. "But that's not what I want." God help her, but she spoke the truth. She wanted him with a fierceness that had never possessed her before. She had to deliver one heck of an authentic performance for this undercover operation.

"I can't give you what you want," he said.

"There's a difference between can't and won't." She reached the other side of the bed, right at crotch level. He was definitely into this, despite what he said. Those cotton sleep pants didn't do a thing to disguise his erection. And all she had to do was get them off him...

"And I see exactly what I want," she said, reaching for his drawstring. She almost had her fingers on it—the drawstring that was—when he jumped back, taking cover behind the chair next to the table.

Oh, great. He was going to make her really work for this. "You're being selfish and inconsiderate. Do you know what happens when Nick doesn't play fair?"

"Serena goes home?" he asked with wry hopefulness. She met so few criminals with a sense of humor.

She rose to her knees on the mattress and reached behind her and grabbed her handbag. "No, I'm not going home and you don't really want me to. Don't play coy with me." She pulled out the short leather quirt with the split leather on the end. "You know what happens when Nick doesn't do what he's told to do."

"Uh, what are you planning to do with that?"

He looked nervous. She supposed that was part of the excitement for him.

She slapped it against her leg and managed not to wince. Ow. That stung. She'd do what she needed to do, but she'd prefer not to actually wield it. "That depends on how cooperative you are. I can do several things with it."

She stroked the end of the whip in one hand, fondling the thicker end suggestively. Then she licked the split leather ends deliberately. It was meant to arouse Slick Nick, but she felt a sensual tightening in her body that had nothing to do with her job and everything to do with her and him and the sexuality that flowed between them like an electric current. She twirled her tongue around one of the thin leather strips, drew it into her mouth and sucked on it.

Nick closed his eyes as if the sight was too painful for him to watch. He clutched the back of the chair, his fingers white where he gripped it.

He opened his eyes. "Please don't do that."

"What?" She deliberately swiped her tongue along the whip's shaft and felt a surge of sexual excitement and power.

"That." He swallowed convulsively. "Could you please get it away from your mouth? Please?"

"You asked nicely, so I'll grant your request. I suppose if you'd rather I did something else with it…" She trailed the damp strips over the exposed tops of her breasts, enjoying the sensation. She dragged the tip along the laces that held her corset together and down her belly. Each slide of the damp leather over her skin sent little shock waves of pleasure and arousal through her.

"No…please…"

She teased the moist leather over the tops of her thighs, along the edge of her fishnets. She eased the tip up the edge of fabric posing as a skirt and along the crotch of her panties. The sensation rocked through her and she forced herself to focus on his reaction. The sooner she got this over with, the better.

"Take off your pants, Nick," she commanded.

NICK COULD barely breathe. Women seemed to like him. They often pursued him, but he'd never had an experience like this. "I told you I wasn't going to have sex with you."

"I understand that. No sex. No kissing." She touched the split ends of her quirt to her neck and her eyes reflected the promise of carnal pleasure. "There's a whole range of other things available."

If he hadn't set himself up with this stupid bet, he wouldn't be hiding behind this chair like some quaking virgin. He'd be touching and tasting and generally working them both toward a satisfactory outcome. But none of that was allowed. Unfortunately he wasn't thinking too clearly. His brain seemed to be fogged with what he couldn't have— which was Serena Barton, one very hot package. They were both getting off on this, but it couldn't go anywhere, he reminded himself. "Give me one good reason I should take off my pants for you."

"Take off your pants and if I like what I see, I may let you take off my boots…with your mouth."

That nearly banished all rational thought in one fell swoop. Those incredible legs, those hot boots, the satin skin beneath those fishnets against his face. Maybe he needed to expand the way he thought, not worry about the destination and just enjoy the journey, even a dead-end journey.

AJ had specified no groping, but groping involved hands. If he used his mouth and teeth, that wasn't technically groping.

He devoured her with his eyes. He'd never burned for a woman the way he burned for her. Women had been something akin to a recreational sport. Serena was more along the lines of a necessity. There'd been something different about her, different about him, from the first moment he'd seen her at the bar. "So, I lose the pants and win the boots. Is that the way it works?"

"You're a quick study."

"And what if you don't like what you see when I take off my pants?" He'd never had any complaints before, but she had thrown in that caveat, *if I like what I see.*

She was looking at him like he was a juicy filet mignon and she had a serious protein deficiency. God, it was hot in here.

He must be out of his mind to seriously consider getting naked for this woman decked out in black leather and sporting a whip. But it wasn't as if he'd picked up a stranger in the bar…well, not exactly. She did know AJ, indirectly, so this was really more like…a blind date.

How had AJ known that she'd strike a chord in him? Float his boat? Start his engine? It didn't really matter how AJ knew, the bottom line was she was here, she was hot, and she had him turned up to a combustible level.

She got off of the bed and closed the gap between them, stopping on the other side of the chair. She smelled incredible—perfume, leather and musky arousal.

"Let go of the chair, Nick." Her voice was low and husky and authoritative. She definitely had control issues—as if the whip and dominatrix outfit hadn't clued him in earlier. He relinquished his hold on the upholstered back. She gripped the arms and moved it aside with apparent ease. He noted her sleekly muscled arms, which got him off even more.

Her scent infused the air; it was as if she was a part of every breath he drew. In those do-me-now, stiletto-heeled boots, her head came to his shoulder. At close range gold and caramel flecked her brown eyes, and freckles dusted her nose. Her mouth was a sensual playground. He could spend hours kissing that mouth, nibbling the fullness of her lower lip, tracing his tongue against the pouty line of the upper curve.

She delicately licked the end of the leather, like

a cat cleaning its paws. Then she whispered the moist ends over his neck, across his chest. All his muscles clenched. All his nerve endings came alive.

She teased the damp tip across his flat male nipple. It was as if an electric jolt traveled from his nipple to his balls, trailing fire in its wake. He groaned aloud. Her smile was pure satisfaction and wicked seduction.

"You're either in the game or you're not," she said. "You don't want to play? That's okay. But if you don't make a decision in the next thirty seconds, then I'm out the door. You don't have to bury your face between my thighs and work my boots down with your mouth. I understand if you're not interested. But the price of admission to this particular party is taking your pants off. If you still want me to go I'll leave you and Sheila alone."

She was good. She was damn good. Nick trembled with want. He'd beat AJ at his own game and have a good time to boot. There was one thing they'd get straight up front, she wasn't going to hit him with that whip.

"No wielding that whip."

"That sounds like a guilty conscience talking. It sounds to me like Nick's been naughty and thinks he needs a spanking."

"No spanking."

"I'll be the one to decide that."

He wasn't sure exactly what AJ had told Serena

about him, but this chick was obviously into the S&M scene—and he wasn't, or at least he never had been. He really should just tell her to leave. Go. Out the door. But there were a couple of reasons he didn't. Numero uno, she was hot. Really, really hot. Second, call him a fool, but he thought he'd really enjoy the sweet torture of peeling those boots down her luscious legs. And third, if she did hit him, how much damage could she do? He probably outweighed her by sixty pounds or so. If she wanted to play some game where he was her love slave, well, he'd go for that. They'd play her domination game…for now.

"Then we need to have a safe word."

Her eyes gleamed with a mix of triumph and acknowledgment. "Name it."

"Brake."

"Brake?"

"Yep."

"Brake it is. Now take your pants off for me, Nick."

She was spectacular, with her legs spread in a stance of a comic book siren. He'd been addicted to comic books as a kid. It was still a guilty pleasure. His hands shook as he untied the drawstring of his pants. They dropped and puddled around his feet.

She stepped back, the better to see him. Her gaze singed him as it licked across his naked flesh. She reached out with her whip and smoothed it over the top of his cock. The blood drained from his head, every nerve ending in his body seemed centered in his engorged tip. She glided the split leather tip down his shaft, the sensation tightened his balls, and then she stroked the tip of the whip over his scrotum and twirled the leather strips so that they tickled the underside of his cock and the top of his balls at the same time.

The sensation…was…incredible. Nick fisted his hands and held on to the control she was destroying with that whip. "Very, very nice…so far. Now turn around."

If that had been a sample of things to come…Nick turned around.

5

SERENA NEARLY DROPPED HER whip. Where was the tattoo? She blinked. There wasn't even a remote sign of a tattoo—no heart, no MOM, no nothing—just tight, gorgeous, to-die-for buns.

She must've uttered a protest because the man who was not Slick Nick Malone glanced over his shoulder. "Is something wrong?"

Was something wrong? Was something freaking wrong? Only that she'd been chasing the wrong man around the room with a riding crop. Other than that, everything was peachy keen.

This was a really bad time to realize Harlan Worth was right and she should always have a backup plan. But she'd been so sure he was Slick Nick—right height, age, weight, hair color, eyes. In the right place at the right time. Harlan had considered Debi Majette credible. How could he *not* be Slick Nick? But there it was, right in front of her, bare-booty proof that he wasn't.

"I'm speechless at the view," she said, which was pretty much true. She needed to keep up the pretense until she could graciously leave. She could hardly throw down her quirt and announce she was outta here.

He grinned over his shoulder, "So, now I get to take off your boots. That was the deal."

This man really was a guy named Nick O'Malley. He hadn't been playing with her or falsely protesting when he told her he didn't want her to spank him. And she had, in fact, promised he could pull her boots off with his teeth, never thinking it would get this far. Thank goodness she hadn't promised anything more…intimate.

"Right. You…can pull my boots off."

So, why had he gone along with her if he wasn't into domination?

He turned around. A sexy smile teased at the corner of his lips and knocked her pulse out of whack. "I'm looking forward to it."

The answer stared her in the face—well, not exactly the face, but it was right in front of her. Men were consummate liars, but not even the best of them could fake a hard-on. This guy was digging her.

Standing around basking in the sex appeal of O'Malley, it occurred to Serena that it was far too coincidental that this guy resembled Slick Nick Malone—all the right physical characteristics, except that he wasn't sporting a tattoo…or a tiny tot.

Serena didn't believe in coincidence. Nix the leaving in five minutes. She'd shift gears, but this had to tie in with Slick Nick somehow. She just had to figure out how. She was missing something. She'd play this out as another lead that had dropped in her lap. Something was definitely up— well, besides his johnson.

This could work. Him taking off her boots bought her time to come up with a new plan. They hadn't taken that long to put on, so they shouldn't be that hard to pull off. Three, maybe four minutes, five at the max. She'd work out her plan and not get caught up in the experience.

Except that smile, that six-pack, but most of all…that mouth. Sexy. Sensual. Dangerous. Hello, libido. No. Think work. It'd be infinitely better for her concentration and overall peace of mind if he didn't put those chiseled lips anywhere near her thighs.

Maybe they'd bend the rules and hurry things along a bit. "Feel free to use your hands," she said.

"Oh, no. Using my teeth is a much better option." His gaze sizzled over her legs. "I'd be much too tempted to touch, if I was using my hands that could technically be misconstrued as groping. And I have no intention of losing on a technicality."

Lose what? Now that she knew he wasn't Nick Malone, she was a little more curious about who this AJ was and what was going on between them. She knew now when he'd said he wasn't going to kiss her or sleep with her, it hadn't been some "no really means yes" ploy of a man who liked to be dominated, so she'd guess he and his buddy had some sort of no-sex wager going.

"I promise I won't tell if you use your hands," she said.

"But it wouldn't be nearly as much fun as using my teeth." He grinned, his teeth gleaming against the dark stubble beginning to shadow his jaw.

He'd neatly turned the tables on her. And she didn't want to have fun. Nope. Just Say No To Fun was her working motto. And that was the problem. She could see herself having far, far too much fun.

"I could handcuff your hands behind your back for you." She had her police-issue cuffs in her handy-dandy bag. And a man with his hands cuffed behind him was a lot less of a threat, although this guy didn't seem threatening at all— except to her peace of mind and her libido.

"Sorry, honey, you don't know me that well." His blue eyes sparkled with blatant sexuality and bad-boy mischief. Nick O'Malley inarguably reigned supreme as the sexiest man she'd ever met. "But if you're into that, I'd be happy to hand-cuff you before I start to take off those boots. In fact, it might even up the playing field since I'm naked and you're not. Would you like that?" His voice dropped an octave, full of sensual promise that guaranteed she'd like it.

Serena's heart raced and she flushed with heat from the inside out. She, who had never given a thought at all to handcuffs outside of an arrest, thought she just might enjoy it with Nick O'Malley. "No. We'll skip the handcuffs."

Something about this man did it for her as no one had ever done it before. Of course, it wasn't as if she'd actually be disappointed if O'Malley announced he had a headache and would rather head to bed than de-boot her with his sexy mouth. Nope. Because then, she, Serena Riggs would have a problem and she didn't have any problems. She only had opportunities. And maintaining her cover, continuing with her role, was a priority.

But what was he going to get out of this? "I know where you stand on the sex thing so if you want to forego taking off my boots, I'll understand."

"No way. I've learned something very important in the last few minutes. Anticipation is the ultimate aphrodisiac." He stepped closer, stopping just short of touching her. Serena struggled to keep a cool head. He was big and naked and there was so much bare skin and heat. He stared at her mouth as if he longed to devour it with his. "I'd rather expire of want than never know the scent of your body and the feel of your skin. That's something AJ'll never understand. It's not about just having sex. It's the journey along the way."

That *was* the sexiest thing she'd ever heard. Definitely the most sensual comment ever directed her way. His words, his nearness, spiked her temperature. She'd seriously slipped in her dominatrix persona. She reminded herself to stay in character. Not only did it protect her cover, but it put a distance between her, the real her, and what was about to happen.

"If you want to take off my boots, kneel on the floor," she said. There. That was much better. She was in control.

"Then, on with the games." Nick dropped to his knees. Maybe she just had a different spin on things now that she knew he wasn't Malone, but there was nothing submissive about this man on his knees.

He didn't touch her. Instead, he planted his hands on either side of her, on the mattress behind her. She stood, the bed pressing against the back of her legs, O'Malley's head level with her thighs. Anticipation arrowed through her, tightening her nipples, slicking her folds, quickening her pulse.

He looked up at her with those intensely blue eyes and she thought it patently unfair any man should possess such dark thick lashes. "I'm going to keep my hands on the sheets. I want you to know that when I'm touching them, I'm thinking about how soft and smooth your skin is."

She had remained calm and steady in the company of vicious drug dealers who would've whored their own mothers to make a deal. She wasn't going to be sent running for the door by a couple of sweet, sexy words murmured by a naked man on his knees in front of her. She was made of sterner stuff than that. Except his words made her quiver inside.

"Okay." She wasn't so sure she could keep her legs steady and utter more than that one word.

Nick nuzzled the inside of her right thigh, his breath warm and arousing against her bare skin. Sensation sizzled along her nerve endings and pooled into a warm, wet welcome between her thighs. Serena made the even worse decision to look down. Seeing his dark head beneath the edge of her ridiculously short skirt was terribly erotic and did nothing to calm her erratic pulse.

"You smell so good. I swear, your scent alone makes me high," he said, his voice muffled, his breath gusting tantalizingly against her with each word.

"That's because I'm hot for you." She hadn't meant to say that. Definitely had not planned to say that. But it was okay, she was just getting into her role. She dismissed the fleeting thought that she just might be in over her head with Nick O'Malley.

For the span of what felt like a lifetime, but was probably only a few seconds, he rested his forehead against her thighs, the crown of his head pressing stimulatingly near her pleasure point, his skin warm against hers, his faint five-o'clock shadow a sensual rasp against her inner thighs. He inhaled deeply and her muscles clenched in an involuntary Kegel.

He exhaled slowly, his breath teasing against her sensitized skin. A plan. She was supposed to be coming up with a plan.

"Oh, Serena, the things I'd like to do to you…for you."

And how was she supposed to think about… whatever she had been thinking about…when he was driving her out of her mind? She knew exactly what she'd like him to do for her. She'd like to lie back on the bed and spread her legs. She wanted him to push her panties aside. She ached to feel the touch of his chiseled lips against her nether lips in an intimate kiss of seduction. She wanted him to lave her wet, eager folds with his tongue, to taste…sample… arouse…probe. She wanted to feel the scrape of his beard against her thighs and the tender skin of her mound. She wanted that marvelous mouth to suckle her until she was nearly screaming with want. And then she wanted to spread her legs, open herself even further to him. She wanted Nick O'Malley to climb on top of her, to pierce her, to drive into her, over and over until she was insensate with satisfaction. Yes. She knew exactly what she wanted…and exactly what she wasn't getting.

"Take off my boots," she commanded.

His smile was nothing short of wicked and she locked her knees to keep herself steady. Who was she kidding? She locked her knees to keep herself upright.

He bent his head and his lips glanced over her skin as he bared his teeth in an almost feral manner and grasped the zipper pull in his pearly whites. He tugged the zipper down from her thigh to just below her knee. He sank his teeth into the top of the boot and inched the leather down her leg, the heat of his skin replacing the supple leather's warmth.

"Spread your legs."

She forgot she was the one who was supposed to be giving orders and did as he said. He angled his head between her legs and once again found the top of her boot. His hair brushed against the damp crotch of her panties. It was a testimony to her fortitude that she didn't melt onto the bed at that instant.

"Wait." She sounded hot and breathless, quite possibly because both applied.

"Is something wrong?"

Yes. Everything was wrong. It felt too good.

"No. I just…um, wanted to know if…you know, if you were uncomfortable. You look uncomfortable down there."

Nick laughed, a warm, sexy rumble. "I'm more comfortable than I've been in twenty-seven days. Great view. To borrow your earlier line, I'm enjoying the scenery. Are you uncomfortable? Would you rather lie down on the bed?"

Flat on her back with this man between her legs? Definitely not. "I'm fine if you're fine."

"I'm at eye level with the loveliest pair of legs I've had the pleasure of meeting. I'm past the point of fine."

"You've got a smooth tongue."

"Ah, if only I could really show you…"

Thank goodness he couldn't. She'd never withstand it. Thank God for whatever crazy rules he and the mysterious AJ had set up between them. His mouth touched her leg again and she barely managed not to winnow her hands through his hair.

Plan. Focus. Concentrate. Rules. No kissing, no groping, no sex. Ahh…his mouth against her… no, no, no, get back to the…whatever it was…oh, yeah, the plan. It had to be a no sex wager. She'd already told him she wasn't a hooker. She needed… oh, yes, when he moved his head like that…no, she didn't need *that*, she needed a cover.

Moisture gathered between her thighs with every nuzzle of his mouth, every bump of his head against her, the press of those shoulders…oh, yes…she needed a sex-related cover…one that fit in with his apparent rules.

Forget it…Nick was blowing her concentration and very possibly her mind. He'd worked her boot down to her knee and now he was tugging it past her knee. He used his nose to nudge it further down.

How could she have made it through twenty-eight years without knowing how exquisitely sensitive the back of her knee could be? How incredibly delicious a gust of warm breath against that part of her body could feel? How the faint scrape of whiskers against nerve endings could melt her from the inside out? She moaned in the back of her throat—an involuntary expression of arousal and satisfaction and entreaty.

The muscles in his arms bunched and corded as he fisted his hands in the sheets. This need he'd awakened in her was like a sickness and he was the cure. Cure…that was exactly the plan. She'd been sent to cure him. She was a sex therapist. It could work.

"I've never wanted to touch any woman as much as I want to touch you now," he said, his voice low, strained, aroused, his cheek pressed against her leg.

She didn't think she'd actually ever *craved* a man's touch before. But she did now, with every fiber of her being. "Nick…"

She sank to the edge of the bed

NICK'S HEART pounded so hard it echoed in his ears.

"Nick," Serena waved her hand in front of his face, "someone's knocking on your door."

Talk about rotten timing. Or maybe it was great timing. When she'd sunk onto the bed and murmured his name in that husky tone, her musky scent beckoning him to that magic spot between her thighs, his willpower had plummeted. Someone knocking at the door could only be a good thing.

He stood on unsteady legs and pulled on his sleep pants. "Who the hell…? Probably some drunk who misplaced his key."

He looked through the peephole. All he could see was a police officer's bill. Why were the cops here?

He glanced over his shoulder at Serena. "I hope you were serious when you said you weren't a hooker, 'cause it's a cop."

Serena paled. "A cop?"

As if to confirm what he'd just told her, a sharp rap sounded on the door. "Open up. Police."

"Hide," Nick mouthed the word and pointed to the closet and then the bathroom. He was attracted to this woman and he didn't want her arrested even if she was a hooker. If she wasn't and he was in some trouble he didn't know about, he didn't want to get her involved.

But she merely shook her head. "I'm fine. Let them in."

He opened the door and felt like a supreme idiot. He'd only seen the police hat. A leggy blonde stood there in a pair of very brief shorts and a shirt that was unbuttoned with the tails tied beneath her extremely large breasts, a frosty beer bottle wedged in her cleavage. She whipped off the hat and long bleached-blond hair tumbled past her shoulders. She tossed her hair and slanted him a look.

"I'm Officer Candy and I'm here to place you under…" She ran her tongue over her full, bubble-gum-pink glossed lips. "House arrest." She pulled the beer from between her massive breasts and held it out to him, "AJ said to tell you he was sending a beer to the island…whatever that means."

Nick took the beer and grinned. "Did he now?"

How many women was AJ planning to fling at him? His buddy was desperate to win. "Uh, thanks but I'm not really up for house arrest." He handed her the beer. "And you can tell AJ that Nick's still on the wagon."

"All these messages are sort of confusing," she said with a pout, putting the beer back in her cleavage.

Obviously AJ had selected Candy for her bust size rather than her IQ—the former was impressive, the latter wasn't much to write home about.

"It's okay. Anything close to that and he'll get my meaning."

"Aren't you going to ask me in?" She peered around him and tried to wiggle past but he blocked her. He was in trouble. Not even the bodacious bleached blonde Candy interested him like Serena did.

"Sorry. I'm busy right now."

He closed the door and turned to face Serena. She'd moved from the bed to the chair and tugged her boot back up to her thigh. Obviously it was a real mood breaker for one woman when another woman showed up almost naked.

Embarrassment shifted him from one foot to another. First, Sheila, then Serena and now Officer Candy. Thanks to AJ, she must think he was a real prize.

"That wasn't very flattering," Serena said. "I guess she's backup, which means he didn't think I could get the job done."

Something about that didn't sound quite right. "Exactly what job are you supposed to get done?"

"When you said you knew he sent me, I assumed you knew why I'm here. I'm a sex therapist and I specialize in interventions." She twirled the whip between her fingers. "I'm the cure for what ails you."

6

"SEX THERAPIST? INTERVENTION?" Nick said.

Okay. Serena knew it was a little wacky, but the blow-up doll and Officer Candy were pretty outrageous. Not to mention well-endowed. Serena had been relieved Nick hadn't tossed her out on her ear and opted for *house arrest* with Officer Candy.

The whole thing was getting stranger and stranger by the minute. Sitting here impersonating a dominatrix for a man who wasn't the person she'd expected him to be while a stripper showed up at the door pretending to be a cop. Now she'd become a sex therapist on an intervention. Well, it was the best she could come up with on short notice. After tonight, she'd never again go into a situation without a backup plan firmly in place.

"Yes. Friends and family often recognize a problem, while you're still in denial. And because they care about you, they call in expert help."

O'Malley sat on the bed, opposite her chair, and shook his head as if to clear it. "Check me on this. Instead of drug or alcohol interventions, you do sex interventions?"

He looked incredulous. She tried to look sincere. "Exactly. AJ is very concerned about you."

Nick's mouth dropped open and he fell back onto the bed, laughing. He had the most seductive laugh. Of course, this guy made breathing sexy. And it had been infinitely less disturbing when he hadn't been sprawled on the bed. "Butthead."

"Don't be angry with your friend." Amusement, not anger, lit his blue eyes but she used a placating tone and a soothing therapist voice. "He wants to help you."

"Right. He wants to help part me from my money."

Serena crossed her legs, more for modesty than any kind of seduction. There was literally nothing to her skirt. It made Sharon Stone's skirt in *Basic Instinct* look prudish in comparison. "Oh, no. He's footed the entire bill for this intervention."

Nick propped on his elbow, the movement etching his pecs and biceps into mouthwatering relief. He lounged on the bed, totally at ease sitting around bare-chested. And with a body like his, why wouldn't he be comfortable sitting around seminude? She didn't doubt he'd had practice. He was one gorgeous man who probably logged in lots of naked hours with women. He could be an artist's model.

"Exactly what problem do I have that requires the intervention of a sex therapist?" he asked, rubbing his thumb over the comforter in an unconsciously sensual gesture.

Serena dragged her attention away from the motion of his fingers against the fabric. "You might feel he compromised your privacy, but I couldn't help you if I didn't know you have intimacy issues."

A frown marred his brow. "Can you be more specific? In case it escaped your attention, taking off your boots while I was naked felt fairly intimate."

The husky note in his voice and the latent heat in his eyes sizzled through her. Not a second spared her the memory of his warm breath against her thighs, the searing contact of his mouth behind her sensitive knee.

"There's really no delicate way to put this. I know you suffer from erectile dysfunction. And I can help you with this problem."

He laughed. "Does this look dysfunctional to you?" He gestured toward the still-impressive bulge in his loose pants.

"I was told you had a problem keeping it up."

"Honey. Take a look. It's still up." A hint of frustration crept into his voice.

She recalled he'd adamantly told her no kissing, no touching, and no sex when he'd first caught her in his room. "According to my notes, your erectile function is fine until you kiss a woman, touch her or attempt intercourse." She offered him a sympathetic look.

"I am not erectile dysfunctional or whatever you said."

"It's nothing to be ashamed of. It happens to more men than you realize. Sometimes, with problems like yours, a little spanking or bondage helps. Often men with erectile dysfunction suffer from the pressure of having to get it up and keep it up." Hey, for totally off-the-cuff bull, this sounded good. "Performance anxiety, you know. But with someone else in charge, they perform fine."

"I'm telling you…" He shoved his hand through his hair and glanced down in the direction of his equipment. "I do not have a problem."

"You're absolutely right. Problem is such an ugly word. Issue is a much better choice."

"The only issue I have is my choice of friends."

"They're trying to help."

"They're buttheads. Let me tell you what this is really about." He rubbed his hand over the flat plane of his belly and her mouth went dry. She really wished he wouldn't do that. "I was stupid enough to take a bet that I couldn't go thirty days without a woman. I know, that makes me a butthead as well." He smiled self-consciously, obviously embarrassed. "Anyway, it means no sex. No kissing. And my good friend AJ specified no groping. They've been throwing women at me left and right. I guess AJ thought a sexpert stood the best chance of undermining me."

Serena bit back a snort of laughter and fought to keep her expression one of sympathetic understanding. Thirty days without a woman. That was the kind of bet the guys at the station would make. And they'd all be having fits at even a hint of rumor that they couldn't keep it up. But this was too much fun to let go so easily. And if she told him she believed him, there was nothing for her to do but go home and that wouldn't keep her in proximity with him and wouldn't provide any more leads or information. She'd be back at square one—which was where she kept finding herself, again and again, in this case.

"We're trained to deal with denial issues," she said. "You can be honest with me."

Frustration flickered over his face, followed by an expression that sent warning signals firing through her. He sat up and slid to the mattress's edge, which put him in her space. He was one very large, very almost-naked man in very close proximity—disturbing proximity that sent heat flashing through her because she knew exactly what those pajama bottoms concealed.

"Okay, let's assume I have this…issue. Exactly how does this intervention work? How far are you willing to go in therapy?" he said.

Her heart pounded in double time. Nick was calling her bluff. "Ultimately the goal is to resolve your intimacy issues."

He snared her with his blue gaze, his look full of sexual challenge. "How far will *you* go to cure me, Serena? I'm trying to get a handle on the protocol. I'm just another client so it wouldn't be a big deal if I kissed you I suppose. Could I kiss you more than once?" He stared at her mouth and her lips tingled. "Do you kiss back? Is it a sweet, maybe-we-should-get-to-know-one-another-better kiss where my lips briefly touch yours?" She ached. "Or is it a long, hot kiss where your breath becomes mine, where I learn the taste and texture of the inside of your mouth with my tongue?" His voice was a low, sexy croon that resonated through her and evoked an answer she didn't particularly want to give.

His words stole her breath and she yearned for what he'd described. All of it. He hadn't touched her, but she almost felt the press of his lips against hers, the slide of his tongue into her mouth. What was wrong with this picture? He was seducing her without even touching her. She was the one who was supposed to be in charge…in control. She reminded herself she was role-playing, this wasn't personal.

Serena wasn't sure whether Nick O'Malley was playing a game with her or testing her or perhaps a little bit of both. She might not actually be a sex therapist, but she was a cop on a job. She was a calm, cool professional. This wasn't personal at all, no matter how tight she was wound inside, no matter how hot and bothered she was.

"Yes. All of that would be considered therapy. I would kiss you back. In fact, I would recommend quite a bit of kissing, of all kinds. It definitely enhances the anticipation factor."

"Let's say the kissing goes well. What comes next?"

Serena had committed to memory the three things he'd mentioned when he'd first discovered her in his room. No kissing. No touching. No sex.

Serena knew all about power. This guy might be bigger than her, but she had the training and knew the moves to put him flat on his back and incapacitate him within seconds, if necessary. And for backup she had handcuffs and a Glock in her purse, which was within reach. That was power. But she was having a taste of another kind of power. Sexual power. Without a doubt, they turned one another on. And now, she was ready to wield a little sexual power.

"After kissing, if you're still maintaining your erection, we move on to touch therapy." She smoothed her hands over her thighs. Nick watched her, redefining bedroom eyes in her vocabulary.

"Do I touch you or do you touch me?"

"Because part of your therapy is predicated on domination, I decide. Since you responded so well to the boot therapy, I believe the best course of action would be for me to allow you to touch me." The mere thought set her body tingling.

"What would that involve? Where would I touch you?"

Serena was a smart woman. She knew she was playing with fire, but these particular flames fascinated her, drew her to the heat. And absolutely no one could role play better than her. She wasn't just good, she was very good. She could be as bold and sexy as the situation required. "First you would touch my neck and my shoulders…" She smoothed her hands over her skin, finding a sensual pleasure in the heat in his eyes and his indrawn breath. "…my arms." She paused, dragging out the moment, heightening the tension that stretched between them, bound them together. "Then we'd evaluate your progress."

"Do you keep the outfit?" His husky question swept through her.

"We wouldn't go bare…at least not in the first session. That might be too much for you," she added, just to let him know who was in control.

"And if it wasn't?"

"Remember the anticipation you mentioned earlier? If you've maintained your erection, and I think therapy's going well, we'd advance to…bare touches."

"What's your pleasure, Serena? Do you like it hard or do you prefer the softer touch?"

Her nipples stabbed against the metal tips. It was as if his every word translated to a touch, plucking at her sensitive points, flaming the fire raging inside her. Her pulse raged out of control.

"It would probably be best to start with the soft touch and move to something more forceful, and if at any time you thought you were beginning to lose your erection, a few disciplinary actions with my whip might get you back in line and at attention."

"That wouldn't be necessary. It'd be much more effective at keeping things…in line…if you used it the way you did earlier."

She glanced at the full-blown erection tenting the front of his sleep pants. "You're certainly holding up well through our discussion."

"Imagine that." She almost laughed at his wry observation. "Is that all the touching that's allowed?"

"Would you like to touch more of me? Or would you like for me to touch you? What do you feel would benefit you the most?" she said.

He stood in one smooth movement, putting her at eye level with his crotch. "I would definitely benefit from your touch." He moved to stand behind her. He leaned forward and braced his hands on the chair arms, almost, but not quite, touching her. His scent wrapped around her like a lover's touch, an exciting combination of after-shave and male sexual arousal. His body heat surrounded her. She looked at his arms on either side of her—at the lean muscle, the sprinkle of dark masculine hair on his forearms, at his well-shaped hands and blunt-tipped fingers—and her recently discovered inner vixen was off and running. "I can't think of a single inch of my body that I wouldn't like to have your fingers or your mouth on." His breath warmed her right ear and sent a prickle of gooseflesh over her. "You sound so clinical and detached, but you look so hot, smell so good, I don't think there'd be anything cool or remote about your touch."

She didn't feel cool or remote, she felt on fire for him. All she had to do was turn her head and she could touch her lips to the smooth skin stretched over the hard line of his bicep. And if she turned around and knelt in the chair…

She didn't answer. Couldn't answer.

"I would definitely benefit from touching more of you." His breath whispered over the nerve endings of her neck and shoulder, stirred wisps of hair against her cheek. "I'd love to slide my hands beneath that leather and feel the soft skin of your belly, feel your muscles clench and quiver at my touch. I want to test the silkiness of your thighs beneath my fingertips. Would you allow that?"

She ached for the touch he described. "This is all about helping you maintain an erection through the various stages of intimacy…" She wasn't playing with fire anymore, she was standing smack dab in the middle of the flames. Nick O'Malley brought out the latent bad girl in her and she was on fire. She knew, felt it in the heat racing through her veins, that sex between her and Nick O'Malley would be very, very good. "…so, yes, I would allow you to touch me intimately if it wouldn't compromise your erection."

"The only thing it would compromise is my heart rate and my ability not to come then and there."

"Oh. Do you also have a problem with premature ejaculation?"

"If I haven't come yet, you should be assured that it's not an issue. And that brings us to the limits on the sex itself."

"That would be the final stage since that would be the ultimate intimacy."

"Yeah, but specifically, are you limited to intercourse or does oral sex count?" He stepped from behind the chair and crossed his arms over his chest. "I'm just trying to get a handle on the parameters."

He was thick and long and she curled her fingers along the chair's edge to keep from reaching for him, to keep from leaning forward and licking the length of his satin shaft. "Oral sex technically falls somewhere in between touching and actual intercourse."

"Is it part of the therapy?"

"My goal is to maximize your therapy. If you thought you'd like that—" she wet her lips "—we'd try it. If you didn't lose your erection, it would be a step in the right direction," no kidding, "but it wouldn't prove you cured."

"Let me get this straight. I'm only considered cured if we successfully have intercourse?"

She wasn't sure how much more of this she could take.

"I think we should wait and discuss that in tomorrow night's session." She picked up her skirt from the floor and zipped it into place over her micro mini. "We don't want to go too far too fast and compromise the therapy. I think we've made tremendous progress this evening." She put her shirt back on and buttoned it. "When I arrived tonight the first words out of your mouth were no kissing, no touching, no sex. See. You've come a long way in just one evening." She picked up her handbag and walked toward the door.

"You're leaving?" He sounded almost forlorn.

He'd all but kicked her out earlier; now he obviously didn't want her to go. Which meant it was the best possible time for her to leave. She needed to think and she really needed to put some distance between her and Nick to think clearly.

"Yes, I'm leaving. The best time to end the session is while you still have an erection and you can feel good about it." She slipped her whip back into her purse. "One more thing. If you mention me to AJ, he'll deny sending me. It's part of the intervention process."

He shook his head. "I wouldn't give AJ the satisfaction of bringing it up," he said, following her to the door. He reached past her and put his hand on the door, stopping her from opening it, trapping her between all his hard male flesh and the exit. He leaned in close, his lips nearly touching hers, his scent enfolding her. "When will I see you again?" His voice dropped and took on a caressing tone.

Serena was quite sure she'd never wanted to kiss or be kissed and then to take and be taken as much as she wanted it right now. Her heart hammered against her ribs.

"Tomorrow night." Her breathiness betrayed her and she turned the door handle, forcing him to move his arm. She opened the door and stepped into the hallway.

"Serena, wait. How do I get in touch with you?"

She looked over her shoulder at him and smiled, putting herself back in control. "You don't."

SERENA SLID into the once-green, now more of an indiscriminate gray, vinyl booth in the back of McCaffrey's twenty-four-hour diner. She was tired, hungry, confused and generally put out by the case and now this…this…whatever it was she had for O'Malley. Attraction? That wasn't nearly a powerful enough description. Lust? Well, there was that, but it wasn't comprehensive enough.

All she knew was that she needed comfort food. McCaffrey's was comfort food. Not only was the food good, her mom had waited tables in a similar diner in Cleveland and Serena had spent many nights tucked in a blanket in the back office. All the waitresses and the night cook, a giant of a man named Maurice, had doted on her. Serena had always felt safe in the diner, surrounded by the homey smells of real food and endless vats of coffee, the clang of dishes and silverware. And her mom had seemed happy there too, making friends with the other waitresses and pulling in good tips. And then her father had got out of jail and moved them to another part of the city for yet another *fresh start* and that had been the end of that.

"Hey, chickadee. How's it going?" Trixie asked, startling Serena out of her reverie. Trixie, with her lined face, ready smile and eyes that held an underlying sadness, reminded Serena of her mother. She poured steaming coffee into the mug on the chipped Formica table and winked at Serena. "It's fresh and you look like you could use a cup."

"Thanks, Trixie." What she could use was a heavy dose of clarification, professionally and personally, but she'd settle for the coffee. She cupped her hands around the stoneware and brought the fragrant brew to her mouth, blowing on it. McCaffrey's coffee could put you in the burn unit. "How've you been? How's Teddy?"

"I'm fine other than that bunion on my left foot and Teddy's figured it out—" Trixie smiled and shrugged "—at least for now. One day at a time, ya know? Thanks."

Teddy, Trixie's twelve-year-old grandson who lived with her, had decided to try his hand at being a punk—skipping school, staying out late, and, Trixie suspected, a little B&E. Trixie had asked Serena to help in handing down some tough love. Serena'd been more than happy to privately and harmlessly scare Teddy straight. God knows she'd rather do that than arrest him in a couple of years, because once he chose that path, in her experience, he'd be set and sunk in a life of crime.

"No problem. You let me know if Teddy needs a refresher." Serena sipped the coffee.

"I think he's going to be fine. He's not hanging out with that little maggot who likes to call himself Ocho, and he's helping out after school at Paulson's Drug Store. He sweeps the floors, unpacks boxes, stuff like that. And none of this is putting any food in front of you. What's it gonna be tonight?"

Serena might be confused on several fronts, but she at least knew exactly what she wanted to eat. "Open-faced roast beef sandwich and homefries. You got any mushroom gravy?"

"I'll let Big John know it's for you and he'll scare some up. Rough night, huh?"

"A little."

"We've got fresh coconut cream pie."

"Bring it on." Life was short. " In fact, I'll eat that while I'm waiting on the other."

Trixie grinned and winked at her. "Sure thing, chickadee."

While she waited on the pie, Serena pulled her notepad and pen out of her purse. Engrossed in recounting what she had so far, she barely noticed when Trixie brought the pie to the table. She finished listing all the apparent facts and set down her pen.

She'd look it over and try to make some sense of things while she pigged out. She forked up a bite. Creamy custard with flakes of tender sweet coconut and a delicate meringue topping melted against her tongue. She looked over at Trixie and gave her the thumbs-up. "She likes it," Trixie yelled back into the kitchen.

Big John possessed a genius with custard pies and his coconut cream in particular was to die for. She and Big John sometimes swapped recipes, but he wouldn't budge on the coconut cream. One day he'd cave and she'd worm the recipe out of him. In the meantime, she'd enjoy every bite.

She skimmed her notes. Her first thought was the same one she'd had in Harlan Worth's office a couple of weeks ago when Debi Majette's info had been passed along: Debi Majette was a setup who'd fed them info as a red herring. But the bug in that theory was the tattoo…and the little penis. Sure, size was a relative issue, but O'Malley wasn't carrying any *small* point of pride. Just thinking about it sent sparks through her. *So, don't think about it*, she told herself and pulled her attention back to Debi Majette. If Majette had been feeding them, why feed them a piece that didn't fit?

Serena polished off the last of the pie and came at it from another angle. Okay, assuming Majette was legit, how did a guy who fit Malone's description in almost every way turn up on the right day, at the right place, at the right time?

Trixie freshened her coffee and picked up the empty pie plate. "Too bad you didn't like the pie."

"I stopped short of licking it clean for you," Serena quipped back, the sugar and caffeine kicking in. "One day Big John's gonna break down and give me that recipe."

"That or one of us might get desperate and sell it to you. What're you paying?" Trixie asked with a wink.

"Yeah, right. But if I thought bribery would work…"

The other side of the equation hit her like an avalanche. Slick Nick always seemed to be one step ahead of her at every juncture. And when she should've had him this time… Was someone giving Slick Nick the tip off? Was there a mole in the 151st? The thought made her physically ill, the same feeling she'd had in the pit of her stomach when she was growing up and she'd find out her father was going back to jail. Betrayal tended to nauseate her.

"You okay? You don't look so good. What's wrong?" Trixie said, eyeing her like a mother hen.

"I'm fine. Just a little queasy there for a minute."

"Maybe you're pregnant," Trixie said matter-of-factly. Trixie, in her early forties with an almost teenage grandson, took unwed pregnancies in stride.

Surprised, Serena laughed, a burst of genuine amusement. "Only if you can get pregnant from thinking about sex." She had a very clear picture of O'Malley standing in front of her, big, lean, hard and aroused and then between her legs, unzipping her boot with his teeth. Instant hot flash. "If that's the case, then put me down for twins."

"You'll make a good mother. You could handle twins."

Was Trixie trying to give her a total panic attack? "I was kidding, Trix. No thanks. I work weird hours in a job where I spend most of my time with society's dregs. I don't even have a dog or a cat. I have a goldfish and a plecostomus." Compliments of the Bennigan family last Christmas. She'd sort of gotten used to them being there when she got home every day.

"A pleco-what?"

"A sucker fish. He sucks the slime off the bowl to keep it clean."

"Two pets. It's the need to nurture."

"Trust me. I don't cuddle my fish." She didn't mention that she often talked to them.

Trix assumed the position, hands on hips. "Tell me about them. What are their names?"

"The plec is sort of a mottled gray-brown, really ugly, and as I said, he sucks the slime off the bowl. His name is Sucka. The goldfish is sort of orange colored and his name is Mutha."

Trixie shook her head. "Mutha. Sucka. Let's hope you don't get a third fish. I'd have to wash your mouth out for what you'd call it."

Actually, she'd thought it was sort of funny in a street slang kind of way and Bennigan's two boys had howled. Serena laughed. "The bowl's only big enough for two."

"Drink your coffee before it gets cold," Trixie admonished her.

Serena didn't point out that she couldn't drink and carry on a discussion about immaculate conception and fish at the same time. Trixie left her with her coffee and her theory that was so painful to think about she'd rather resume her inane conversation.

If this theory was right, and all the pieces fit, who was it? To have access to case information, it had to be someone in their immediate department. Anxiety churned in her gut.

Harlan Worth's wife had been driving a brand-new Cadillac the last time Serena had seen her. Serena had wondered about it at the time. A new luxury car was no small monetary feat with their two kids in college.

Pantoni's divorce wasn't amicable. Francesca was apparently taking the kids and the house unless Joe coughed up a cash settlement. Bennigan had a troubling affinity for the craps tables. Mike Harding's wife, Becca, liked jewelry—nice, expensive jewelry. And last but not least, Steve Shea had an aging mother who required constant medical care—not a cheap endeavor. Heck, for that matter, if anyone was looking for people with financial needs, she'd be suspect as well, since she was saving every penny toward a down payment on a house.

Bottom line, she'd yet to meet a cop whose pay

covered his or her financial needs. No one took on police work because it was fiscally rewarding.

She didn't want it to be true, in the worst kind of way. These guys had become family, more so than the family she'd walked away from eleven years ago, but until she had more answers, she couldn't afford to take any chances.

Not since she'd left Cleveland and never looked back had she felt so unutterably, miserably alone. She could take this to no one, share her suspicions with no one.

If she slipped up and confided in the wrong person, she could wind up fish food in Boston Harbor. And quite possibly O'Malley'd be taking that scenic tour with her. Every instinct she possessed screamed O'Malley was an unwitting pawn. Otherwise, he wouldn't have sent her for cover when he thought the police were outside his door, he would've known she *was* the police. But the concern in his eyes had been for her. And if O'Malley wasn't a willing participant in whatever was going down, he was in serious danger.

Trixie slid a steaming platter of roast beef sandwich and homefries in front of Serena. "Uh-oh. Trouble just staggered in."

What? Too many cops frequented McCaffrey's for any trouble to go down. Drunks usually steered clear.

Serena looked at the front door. Pantoni weaved toward her.

Trixie's mouth tightened into a straight line of

worry. "Third time this week he's come in like this. I'll go get the coffee."

He'd been in worse condition New Year's Eve two years ago, but this wasn't good.

"S'rena, mind if I sit with you?"

"Sure, Joe."

Pantoni slid into the seat opposite her. The smell of beer clung to him, as if his overbright eyes and unsteady gait hadn't already given him away. She'd say he was about two beers past sober.

"Mind if I eat while you sit?" Serena asked, suddenly needing a little comfort food more than ever. She forked up a couple of homefries and dragged them through the mushroom gravy. Potatoes and gravy. She was duly comforted.

"G'head. I just wanted some comp'ny. So'd you make Slick Dick tonight?" he asked.

Okay. Maybe he was closer to three beers past sober if he couldn't get the name right. She chewed a mouthful of roast beef. And she'd love to bounce the case off Pantoni, but certainly not when he was tanked. She slipped her note pad back into her purse. "I didn't get a positive ID on him."

"C'mon, you couldn't get him out of his pants to show off his ass and his family jewels? And you in them boots? Maybe instead of a little dick he's got no dick."

Whoa! Time to change the conversation. Pantoni was basically a good guy, but when he was drunk he could be incredibly crude and lewd.

She'd rather talk with her mouth full and cut him off at the pass, so she asked, "Whatcha been up to tonight, Joey?"

He scowled and a sullen look she'd never seen before settled over his features. "I haven't been up to nothin'. I just had a couple of beers at Deano's. You women are all the same. You always think we're up to something when we ain't done nothin'. Why'nt you kiss my ass?"

They went way back and she'd seen him rude and crude a couple of times, but never mean. Drunk or not, torn up over his divorce or not, she'd had enough. "What the hell's your problem?"

"Whas my problem? You couldn't handle my problem." He laughed, the sound totally devoid of his usual good-natured mirth. "You ever done something you shouldn't? Something bad wrong? Something that betrayed people you cared about 'cause your back was against the wall?"

A chill of dread slid down her spine and she pushed away the rest of her meal, her appetite lost. "What're you talking about, Joe? What've you done?"

"I bet you never do nothin' fuggin' wrong. 'Cause you're the right Miz Righteous. I mean the righteous Mis Rightful. Fuggit. You know what I mean."

No, no, no. Not Joe. Please, not Joey, a man she'd always considered to have the utmost integrity.

"Yeah, I know what you mean." Serena steeled

herself against the piercing hurt. She laid enough on the table to cover the bill and a generous tip. The implications behind Pantoni's drunken ramblings left her feeling physically ill.

Serena slipped her purse over one shoulder, and pulled him up and onto her other shoulder, wrapping her arm around him. "Come on, Joey. Let's get you home."

"See ya, chickie," Trixie called from behind the counter. She shot both Serena and Pantoni a worried look.

"See ya, Trix. We're fine."

They'd only made it halfway down the sidewalk when Pantoni stopped, forcing her to stop as well. "Ya gotta believe me that I never meant to hurt you, S'rena. Never wanted to hurt you. You're like my sister, but I like you better than my sisters. Fuggit, I never meant to hurt you."

Did he mean his earlier belligerence or did he mean something more insidious like betraying the whole department?

"What did you do?"

But he just slumped against her and stumbled along beside her.

She wouldn't have an answer tonight, but she'd find out the truth and soon. Tomorrow she'd learn everything she could about Nick O'Malley before she met him again at The Barrister. And in the meantime, she'd keep her eyes and ears open and her mouth shut in the department.

7

THE FOLLOWING AFTERNOON NICK paced his room,
impatient and frustrated. He had way too much
time on his hands to sit around and torment himself with thoughts of Serena Barton and the things
she'd done with her riding crop and the things
he'd like to do with her, to her, for her. Sitting
around with a raging hard-on wasn't his idea of a
good time. He looked over at Sheila.

"I need something constructive to do, Sheila
my love. Don't give me that look, you ingenue. I
think you and I should agree to just be friends. I'm
calling Harv."

Surely Harv, his immediate supervisor, could
find something to occupy Nick's time and mind.
He tapped his fingers on the tabletop while he
waited to be patched through.

"Harv here." Harv's smooth, well-modulated
tone always reminded Nick of his Uncle Patrick,
an undertaker with a thriving business in Salt Lake
City.

"Hi, Harv. Nick O'Malley here. Just wanted to
check in with you."

"Nick, everything going okay?"

"Absolutely. No problems." Sure. If you didn't count it being a waste of Mack Enterprises' time and money to pay him to sit around doing nothing. He offered Harv a more positive spin. "You know I really think this could be handled with a couple of phone calls. I was checking in to see if you wanted me to work on something more or just check out and deal with it over the phone."

"Nick, I'm very impressed with your dedication, but don't worry about it. Relax. Catch a couple of movies on cable. Order room service."

"I just thought I'd save the company a few bucks for the room and food if I handled the business with a few phone calls from the office."

"Oh no. You stay and have a good time. You being there is good PR for the company."

Good PR? For who? The hotel? "All right then."

"I knew you were a company man the first time I met you, Nick. Keep up the good work."

Nick hung up and leaned back, balancing his chair on two legs. Either Harv thought Nick was stupid, or lazy—or perhaps both—which really wasn't anything new for Nick.

All his life people had underestimated him. His big brother, Rourke, had always been so serious, so somber, so smart, and God help him, when they were kids Rourke had definitely looked the part with buck teeth and Coke-bottle glasses. Rourke hadn't just looked nerdy, he had been a living, breathing geek personified. The whole world looked at Rourke and knew he was smart and told him he was smart. Was there a kid alive who didn't want to be like their big brother? Nick had looked up to Rourke and wanted to be just like him.

But people looked at Nick and pinched his cheeks and told him how cute he was. Early on Nick had been slotted as the "dumb blonde" of the O'Malley family. Nicky was cute so they didn't expect too much from him. And Nicky had delivered on that expectation. He'd spent a lifetime loving, longing to be and resenting his older brother. And then it had all culminated in him embezzling the money. No one had ever figured out that it wasn't about the money. He could've covered his tracks and no one would've ever figured it out. He'd wanted to be caught. He'd wanted everyone to know that he, Nicholas Patrick O'Malley was smart enough to steal half a million bucks. What he hadn't counted on was the impact on his family. What he'd done had been the height of irresponsibility and immaturity and he regretted it on a daily basis. He'd pretty much come to accept that he'd live with the regret for the rest of his life. And he'd also realized that he didn't have to play down to people's expectations.

So, whereas sit back and rent a movie and have a good time might've worked for him at one point, it didn't now. People only underestimated him if he allowed them to. And something smelled rotten in Denmark. The problem was, he wasn't quite sure what to do about it. He couldn't afford to walk away from a decent job without anything more substantial. What was he going to say, "Oh, hey, Mom, Dad, I quit that job because it seemed sort of fishy that they weren't expecting enough from me"?

He plunked the chair back down onto all four legs. His fingers hovered over the keyboard. It'd be so easy to hack into Mack Enterprises, do a little fishing, check things out. But if he got caught… No one would believe he was simply checking up on the company. Hell no. Everyone would assume he was trying to pull another stunt like before. No way he was doing something risky like that. He wasn't even going to take the chance. He never intended to find himself in a situation where he needed to be bailed out again. And he never wanted to see that kind of disappointment in his parents' eyes again. Forget it. No hacking. Not even to cover his butt.

"Okay. So, it looks as if it's just you and me until Serena shows up tonight," he said to Sheila. Serena was a kindred spirit. With her girl-next-door looks and wide brown eyes that hid secrets, Nick was sure Serena wasn't what she seemed. And he also felt sure people underestimated her. "Let's see what we can find on Serena Barton."

Several keystrokes later he knew exactly what he'd known before. Not much. There were three listings for S. Barton in the greater Boston phone numbers, but no Serena, which didn't surprise him at all. Lots of single women didn't put their first name in the phone listings. No sex therapists Web site, no domination Web site. Of course, that didn't really mean anything.

She might be a dominatrix—she had an underlying "I'll kick your ass if you mess with me" attitude—but he wasn't sure about the sex therapist. The hitch in her breathing, the responsive flicker of heat in her eyes when he'd told her what he wanted to do to her left him wondering.

The other thing that had occurred to him once he was thinking with the head on his shoulders, rather than the one between his legs, was that even though AJ liked to win, he was cheap. He'd spring for a strip-a-gram from Officer Candy and maybe he'd throw some money out to a friend of a friend who was into domination, but Nick wasn't convinced AJ'd shell out bucks for a professional sex therapist. And there was one more detail that niggled at him that he couldn't quite put his finger on, but, bottom line, Serena Barton wasn't who or what she seemed to be.

Regardless, she had him tied up in knots.

SERENA CLIMBED the worn, dark-red brick steps of the 151st precinct, taking care to avoid the loose brick on the third step. She entered the building with its mix of smells: worn wooden floors, a meatball sub someone had heated up for a late dinner and the stench of sweat—criminals brought in off the street weren't always particular about their hygiene. Yet she'd turned down a transfer last year to a bright, shiny new station.

The 151st could've been the stage set for one of those gritty police dramas. In her mind it looked how a police station should look. She'd never told anyone because they would've done something stupid like accuse her of sentimentality, but the 151st was a familiar, known quantity. The 151st was home.

"Hey, Jimmy, how's Dylan?" she asked the gray-haired giant behind the scarred wood counter fronted by floor-to-ceiling bulletproof glass.

Jimmy's eyes lit up, pleased at the opportunity to discuss his greatest joy in life—his towheaded, twenty-month-old grandson.

"He's a firecracker, that's for sure. Got some new photos if you've got a minute." He was already reaching for the envelope on his desk.

"Always."

She oohed and ahhhed appropriately, which really wasn't a hardship because the kid was a cutie. She silently laughed at herself as she recalled how it'd taken her months to figure out Jimmy was the station patriarch and not some pervert. With her own father doing time more often than not, fatherly interest and concern had been a whole new experience for Serena.

She glanced at the final photo of Dylan in a pull-up, wearing a cowboy hat and a bad attitude. "He's a pistol, all right."

"That he is." His grandfather tucked the last

picture back into the envelope with an indulgent smile. "When are you gonna settle down and give your folks a grandkid or two?"

She stared at Jimmy. What was it with everyone throwing babies her way?

"What? Can't a grandpa ask?" Jimmy said.

"I have fish," she said, knowing full well he'd find that answer inadequate.

"Oh, brother." He tucked the envelope into a drawer. "What's the cover tonight?" He eyed her black spandex dress. "Not quite flashy enough for prostitution."

"Dominatrix."

"There you go." He laughed. "You women are used to ordering us men around. Shouldn't be a stretch."

Serena laughed along with him and moved toward the stairs leading to the second floor. "See ya later, Jimmy."

She'd shown up at the station several times before, wearing various disguises. Undoubtedly she had grief coming her way over the red stiletto heels and the curve-hugging dress that was split thigh-high on one side. She had no idea how real women wore these shoes every day. Her feet were killing her, but even she had to admit the outfit pushed her sexy factor up about a gazillion notches. The black lace thong and the push-up bra hadn't hurt either.

Nor had thinking about O'Malley. Something she'd found fairly impossible not to do, which would have been all good and fine had she been thinking about him from the standpoint of how he fit into the case. And she had been thinking about him in a professional way. But then she'd get this crazy butterflies-in-her-belly feeling. She'd remember the way he'd described kissing her, and the feel of his warm breath against her neck, the low timbre of his voice and the smoldering heat in his eyes when he'd said what he wanted to do to her, and she'd pretty much melt inside like a two-scoop cone on a hot summer day.

At the top of the stairs she veered to the left. Even from here, Bennigan's noxious cigar permeated the air. It always struck her as ironic that laws prohibited the average person from lighting up in a public place, but everyone at the station had to endure Bennigan's cigars. Would Joe even remember what he'd said to her at McCaffrey's last night? He'd been pretty trashed.

She walked into the room and stopped by her desk to thumb through her messages. Nothing that couldn't wait until she was out of Worth's office. She headed in that direction, dreading the meeting, needing to get it over with.

Pantoni hung up his phone. "Ho Mama, bring some of that over here," he yelled across the room. He obviously didn't recall their conversation and he obviously wasn't suffering a hangover.

These guys were so predictable. At least she'd thought so until yesterday 'cause she'd certainly never predicted one of them would rat out the department.

"Walk this way, baby, and I'll show you who's your daddy," Brian Bennigan called out.

She turned to face them and smiled sweetly. "Neither one of you boys could handle it." And that was exactly what they expected from her.

Serena knocked on Worth's office door, abandoning Pantoni and Bennigan to good-natured ribbing. If one of them had sold her and her case down the river, it didn't show on their faces.

She walked in and closed the door behind her. She'd interpret it as a sign of the Second Coming the day she walked in and Harlan's desk was anything less than paperwork chaos.

Sitting on the other side of the organizational fiasco, Harlan did a double take. "That's some getup. I always feel as if I should send you back home to put on more clothes when you're dressed like that."

Surely a guy who acted like a protective uncle wouldn't betray their department. She forced a laugh. "No can do. I've got this undercover assignment as a dominatrix."

"And I thought you were heading out to teach Sunday school." Worth grinned. "How'd last night go? Did our boy show up?"

Serena had rehearsed this conversation in her head all afternoon. "He did. And I made contact."

Without being overt, she watched Worth's facial expression carefully, just as she'd watched every guy when she'd come through the bullpen.

Sleep had been a long time coming last night and she'd turned the case over and over in her head. Unfortunately she'd kept reaching the unhappy conclusion that someone was filling Slick Nick in on the game.

Harlan fished out a Twinkie. "Did you get a look at his ass?"

She threw her hands up. "What? You think I can just waltz up to the guy and he'll show me his buns?"

Harlan smirked. "If you were wearing that, yeah."

"It's not quite that easy. But I'm supposed to meet him again tonight and I'll definitely be working on it." She definitely *wouldn't* be working on getting O'Malley out of his pants. Just thinking about it made her heart pound. She'd been there, done that, and it was a dangerous walk, full of sensual temptations. She needed information and planned to tell him their therapy tonight involved her getting to know more about him. "Any new developments?"

Harlan shook his head. "You'd have been the first to know."

"What about Debi Majette?"

"What about her?" Harlan gave her a disgruntled look.

"Can I have her contact information?"

He leaned back in his ancient office chair, the

springs groaning in protest. "Why would you need that?"

"So I can coordinate a positive ID once I get a look at my man's butt." So she could evaluate Debi's credibility firsthand.

"You don't need to worry about that. Haul in Slick Nick and I'll take care of him."

Serena shrugged while inside her gut churned. She could hardly press the issue without raising Harlan's suspicions. Please, God. Not Harlan Worth.

"Don't worry, I'll bring Slick Nick in for you," she said.

"I'm counting on you," Harlan said. He proceeded to fill her in on two other cases she'd been the lead detective for and when she could expect to make a courtroom appearance on behalf of the great state of Massachusetts. "So, that about covers it," Harlan concluded.

Serena stood and forced a smile. "Time for me to work on getting our boy out of his pants," she said for Harlan's benefit.

"Five to one says you'll hit pay dirt wearing that outfit."

The idea left her weak-kneed.

NICK COVERED the rest of his chicken and pasta with the plastic lid and set the tray out in the hall for pickup. He'd been so strung out last night from sexual tension that he hadn't asked Serena what time she'd be back tonight. And he damn sure didn't want to miss her by going down to the restaurant, so he'd ordered room service.

He ducked into the bathroom and brushed his teeth. He was all kinds of a fool to be so torqued about seeing her this evening.

What he should do was make sure he was conspicuously absent when she showed up tonight, steer clear of her for the next couple of days. When he'd won his bet, he'd find and cozy up to a woman who didn't destroy his composure.

The problem was, he didn't want just any woman. He wanted Serena.

If he didn't do the smart thing and run screaming in the other direction, as soon as he'd won his bet, he should sleep with her and then be on his merry way.

The very last thing he should do, the least intelligent choice, the decision that bordered on lunacy, would be to go along with her, to pretend he had some crazy intimacy issues just as a way to spend time with her. However, his alter ego argued, he'd tried to convince her he wasn't sexually dysfunctional and had gotten nowhere, so why not roll with it? And it undisputedly opened the door to more intimate conversation. He was curious about what was inside her head.

He'd never felt this way before—supercharged, energized, edgy, consumed by a woman. That analogy fit. Thoughts of Serena had consumed him today.

He checked his watch. He really should have

pinned her down to a time. It had been late when she'd arrived last night. That had been quite a surprise, waking up and finding her in his room with those incredible boots and those legs. He smiled at the thought. What a bizarre turn of events.

Something odd about last evening—odder than having a woman turn up in his room uninvited— niggled again at the back of his mind. He'd been asleep when she'd woken him, but it was an oddity in the sequencing that bothered him. The click of the lock had awakened him and there she stood. The click of the lock…then she was there… The thing that didn't belong, well, rather, the thing that belonged but was absent suddenly struck him. What about the light from the hall? Illumination from the hallway should have followed the lock's click. And she should have been facing him. But she'd been facing the door, hadn't she? So, that would mean…

A knock at the door interrupted his thoughts. Anticipation raced through him, set his heart thumping a little harder. Everything was so mixed up—most of all him. He crossed the room and checked his appearance in the mirror, suddenly nervous and unsure of himself. He hadn't known what to wear for an unnecessary sexual intervention. He'd kept on his shirt and slacks, but lost his tie from earlier today.

He opened the door. Serena stood on the other side of the threshold, mind-blowing in a black dress and red stiletto heels.

"I'm back."

"Come in." He stood aside. She stepped past him, his body humming like a tuning fork when her arm brushed against him. She smelled good, too. Some women wore far too much perfume or opted for heavy scents. Serena smelled light and sexy. Nick wanted to bury his face in her neck, breathe in her scent, surround himself with her bewitching fragrance.

Instead, he closed the door behind her. She turned to face him and instinctively he reached for her. His fingers were mere inches from her face when he caught himself. He fisted his hand and shoved it by his side.

She looked up at him and he could barely breathe. "Nick…I meant…to come earlier." Her words seemed to bog down in the bewitchment between the two of them. It was the same as it had been last night when he'd first seen her in the bar. That same draw, that same sense of inevitability. Her lashes cast shadows on her cheeks, her lips beckoned—ripe and luscious, vulnerable. He braced his hands on the wall behind her, on either side of her head. He leaned forward and inhaled her scent.

He'd never wanted a mere kiss more than now, with her. He'd slept with women when he felt less longing, less need. It was ridiculous to deny himself over a bet. Who cared if AJ won? Was it really worth five hundred dollars not to kiss this woman? Not to taste her? Was five hundred dollars enough compensation *not* to touch her when he ached to skim his fingers over her face, longed to see if the chemistry, the sizzle, between them last night was mere hype or real?

Doubtless his buddies would say he was stupid or weak. Who the hell cared?

He cupped her head in his hands and stroked her temples with his thumbs. Her lips parted. Her eyes widened. His heart damn near beat out of his chest.

"Serena…"

"Nick…" She covered his hands with hers. "Are you sure you want to do this?"

He lowered his head a fraction, drawn to her. What she was didn't matter. He wanted her. "I've never been surer."

He gentled his lips over hers. It was like taking a long, slow drink on a hot day—just what he wanted, but it didn't quench his thirst. He kissed her longer and harder and she kissed him back, opening her mouth. He swept the tender recesses with his tongue and learned her taste and her texture.

She wrapped her arms around his shoulders, her hands splayed across his back, pulling him closer, her tongue responding to his teasing with a sensuous play of her own. Her touch, her taste, her scent ignited him. All the heat she'd generated in him last night had merely smoldered today, waiting for her to fan the flames.

Nick had always been as laid-back in the bedroom as he was in the rest of his life, but Serena incited an urgency he'd never known before. He knew for sure it wasn't twenty-nine days of going without. This hunger drove him from inside. He wanted to devour her, to get under her skin, as if by kissing her deep enough, hard enough, somehow he'd be privy to the secrets behind her eyes.

He pulled back, his breath harsh and irregular. Her eyes glittered with a heat beyond arousing.

She reached between them and feathered her fingers beneath his shirt. Cool air rushed against his heated skin.

She trailed her lips down his neck to his chest, nipping, lapping, her tongue finding the sensitive hollow of his throat. Her mouth was wet and warm against him; her hair tickled against his skin. She paused and looked up at him. "Sorry about your bet."

He dragged in a harsh breath. "What bet?"

She laughed, low and seductive, and swept her hand between them, sliding it along his erection. "You've passed the kissing and touching portion of the therapy with flying colors. What do you say to a crash course?"

He cupped her buttocks in his hands and pulled her against him, lifting her off the ground and grinding her hips against his hard-on. She ground back and he leaned her against the wall, letting it support some of her weight while he kissed her, his tongue in her mouth, his hands on her bottom, his erection throbbing between her thighs.

She wrapped her arms around his neck and her legs around his waist, opening herself, bringing him that much closer to where he ultimately wanted to be. She sucked his tongue into her mouth and he felt the pull, all the way to his balls. God, he could almost explode.

While she teased him with her mouth, he reached between them and filled his hands with her breasts, squeezing and kneading, rolling her nipples between his finger and thumb. He lightly pinched her and she surged her hips against him, moaning into his mouth. His left hand still toying with her breast, he slid his right hand up her thigh, where her dress was split, and up the curve of her butt, finding one bare rounded cheek. Was she commando? He encountered a fabric string. A hot thong.

He moaned his satisfaction into her open mouth and she swallowed it with her kiss. He pulled her dress up to her waist, baring her buttocks and cupped one cheek in each of his hands, plumping them, squeezing, pulling them apart and then pushing them back together again. She went wild and he thrust against her in return. He sucked on her lower lip and she panted and moaned into his mouth. He slid one finger farther down, past the scrap of underwear. She was dripping wet. It certainly answered last night's question as to whether she kissed back and fully participated.

Dragging her mouth from his, she lowered her legs. She leaned against the wall, her breathing harsh, her eyes glittering.

He shoved his hands through his hair, feeling like a total jerk. He'd practically jumped her at the door. "I'm sorry." He gentled the back of his hand over her jaw and she tilted her head into his touch. Her skin felt like warm, supple suede against his knuckles. He traced her cheekbone with his thumb. "I couldn't sleep after you left last night. I've been thinking about you all day, waiting for this moment. I hadn't planned to kiss you." He trailed his fingers down the side of her neck and he felt her tiny shiver. He leaned down and chased that shiver with his lips, testing the warmth and texture of her skin with his mouth. She tasted even better, felt even more right in his arms than he thought she would.

"But you did." Serena slid her fingers through his hair, his scalp tingling where she touched him.

"Yes." He kissed the corner of her mouth.

She moved her mouth just enough to nuzzle her lips against his. "Why?" she breathed into his mouth.

"Why hadn't I planned to kiss you or why did I kiss you?"

"Both."

"I didn't plan to kiss you because that just turned out to be the most expensive kiss I've ever had." He smiled, because he could care less about the money. He'd willingly make the same choice again. And then, her alluring scent a part of every breath he took, he gave her the unadorned truth. "And as to why I kissed you…it's simple. I wanted your kiss more than my next breath."

8

Serena rested her head against the solid warmth of Nick's chest. She had no business being in his arms, exchanging kisses, but when she'd stepped through the door, it had been like discovering a safe port in the midst of a storm. O'Malley wasn't particularly a calm port but he'd felt comforting and solid, which was peculiar considering she'd only met him yesterday. But a hollow aloneness had marked her since she'd figured out last night that one of her fellow cops was a traitor. And then she'd walked into the door and she'd found a haven in his eyes, his scent, his arms, and a sweeping rush of desire had displaced that hollowness.

This wasn't what she'd planned to do when she'd come here tonight. She'd come to gather information. As if they had a mind of their own, her hands slid beneath his shirt and she sucked in her breath at the six-pack abs covered by warm velvet skin and just the right sprinkling of hair.

She was working undercover and should she really be here, doing this? It wasn't the most professional move she'd ever made, but in her professional opinion Nick O'Malley wasn't a suspect, but he might be a lead. And she was a woman.

He made her deliciously aware of being a woman—not that she'd ever had any gender confusion, but with Nick it was a whole new ball game. She was more tuned into herself, her femininity, the power of her sexuality. Would it be better if she didn't fall into bed with O'Malley? Probably.

But the world wasn't going to end if she did. And she fully planned to do just that. If she'd thought he was hot before, he'd moved to a new level of incendiary now. And she wanted him. Now.

"There's a time and a season for everything. At some point in time I want you to cover every inch of my body with your sexy mouth. I want you to suck on my nipples until I scream. I want the slow torture of you everywhere but in me. But now is not that time."

They'd had an entire evening of foreplay the night before and an entire day of waiting for *now*.

O'Malley brushed his thumb over her lip. "I agree. That's next time."

He kissed her, hot, drugging kisses, while he walked backward across the room until they reached the bed. She stroked him and he surged against her hand. She was wet and aching with the need to have him between her thighs, stretching her, filling her. He stepped back and pulled her dress up over her head, then tossed it onto the floor.

While Nick got naked, she reached behind her

and unhooked her bra. She slid it over her arms and let it drop to the floor in front of her. She reached for the black thong and Nick captured her wrists. "Leave it on." His voice was low, commanding, and a thrill ran through her. In her world, she usually issued the orders. He looked at her and the heat in his eyes left her panting. "And the red heels, too."

Never looking away from her, he rolled a condom over the thick length of his shaft. Serena ached in anticipation. He backed her onto the bed and followed her down. She thrilled to the slide of his skin against hers, his weight, the breadth of his shoulders and chest, the power in his arms on either side of her, the heady scent combination of Nick and his aftershave.

She bent her knees, bracing her feet on the mattress and opening her legs in bold invitation. He bent his head and swiped his tongue across one nipple and then the other. The sensation zinged through her, straight between her thighs, arching her back off the mattress. "Yes!"

Nick laughed, that low sexy rumble that left her tingling, as if she wasn't a mass of raw nerves already. "More of that…later."

He positioned himself between her thighs and traced her slit through the drenched material of her panties. She bit her lip to keep from screaming at the touch, which teased but didn't satisfy.

"Serena, you make me so hot and hard. I want to show you just how hard I am for you."

She took him in her hand, guiding him closer

to where she wanted him. "I want you to show me. I'm hot and wet and hungry for you." It only upped her turned-on level by about a thousand to talk to him that way. Apparently it was a big hit for him as well.

He reached around her hip and fisted his hand around the narrow strip of her thong, for a moment pulling it tighter between her drenched thighs, taunting her with its rub against her clit. And then he pulled it aside and in one smooth stroke gave her exactly what she craved, all of him. He pulled almost all the way out and did it all over again. And again. With each thrust, each stroke, she met him, urged him on with her own thrusts. Sweat slicked her skin and she drew her knees closer to her chest and spread her legs farther apart, opening herself as much as possible, eager for everything he was giving her and more. She loved the way his balls slapped against her, the tug of her panties on her vagina, the feel of his fist against her butt.

"Oh, Nick, you feel so good inside me. So hot. So hard." Her breath came in short, hard pants. Every time he drove into her, the tension inside her notched a little higher, tighter, stretching her taut like a string.

He smiled down at her. "I love it when you talk to me that way. And you're so wet and hot, I think you love it, too." He reached between them and cupped her breasts, slowing the pace. He rolled her nipples between his fingers and she felt herself on the brink of shattering. "Come on, baby, tell me what you want and tell me how you want it."

She told him exactly what she wanted and how she wanted it, just the way a good girl wouldn't. "I want you to take me. Hard and fast."

His blue eyes blazed, a sexy smile tilted his lips and he drove into her. "Like this?"

"Oh, yeah…just like that." Deep inside her, she felt the first tremor of her orgasm.

"I want to hear how much you like it," Nick said. He reached between them and, with excellent instinct, homed in on her nub and stroked with his finger while he pumped in and out of her.

Her orgasm rolled through her, ravaged her, all the more intense as she let him know how very much she liked it. And he joined her on the ride, his moans and the sharp breathless way he uttered her name as he came adding to her satisfaction.

She lay spent, satisfied, loving the feel of him still inside her, the weight of him on top of her. He leaned down and with a lazy, satiated smile captured her mouth in a deep, long kiss. She linked her arms around his neck.

This was definitely worth the price of admission.

NICK SAUNTERED back into the room, feeling better than he'd possibly ever felt in his entire life. Serena lay on the bed in a tangle of pillows and sheets and discarded clothes. She'd pulled the sheet up over her, but left her heels on.

"Oh, honey, you've covered up the scenery. And it's such a nice view. It's like being in a Paris apartment with the curtain closed."

"Maybe I don't want you to get tired of the view."

Her apparent modesty amused him, considering what they'd just done. She was definitely a woman of surprises. Who'd expect modesty in a dominatrix?

He'd missed it on his way to the bathroom, but now he saw that in the midst of tearing off clothes and finding satisfaction in each other, her purse had been kicked off of the bed. Her whip and a lipstick case lay on the carpet.

Nick knelt at the foot of the bed and tossed the whip up onto the mattress.

"That could definitely come in handy," he said.

"What are you doing?"

"Your purse fell off the bed." He picked it up to put her lipstick back in. Distracted by memories of how she'd driven him crazy last night tonguing the leather toy, trailing it across her body, he up-ended her shoulder bag, the contents spilling onto the carpeted floor.

"Damn." It took about two seconds for the important items to register: gun, BPD badge, handcuffs. He felt as if she'd just landed a solid kick to his groin. She was a freaking cop.

She lunged for the end of the bed and he stood

up, her weapon in one hand, badge in the other. "Is this what you're looking for?"

"Put the gun on the bed and step away from it. And be careful, it's loaded," she said, all traces of vulnerability vanquished. She was a harsh-voiced, hard-nosed cop.

Nick stared at the weapon. He'd never even touched a gun before and she ran around with a loaded one.

"Now. Put it down *now*," she said.

Nick placed the gun on the mattress and stepped back. She picked up the weapon and trained it on him.

"Does this mean you're not here for a sexual intervention?" A little dose of humor mixed with a touch of sarcasm surely wasn't remiss when he'd just slept with a woman who was now aiming a gun at him.

"Move away from the bed." He took a few steps back and she lowered the weapon. "For future reference, never point a gun at a cop. It's usually not good for someone's health."

Well, hell, he hadn't exactly meant to point it. He was handing it to her. Nick walked over to face the wall, then leaned against it, spread-eagle. "Is this the part where you strip-search me?" He paused for a second and then glanced at her over his shoulder. "Oh, yeah. You've already covered that, haven't you? I'll have to say you were quite thorough. But then you've probably had a lot of practice, haven't you?"

Dammit but he was pissed…and embarrassed. He'd tossed away a five hundred dollar bet and he'd slept with a cop who was probably going to arrest him any minute. And then, greater yet, he'd have to call someone to bail him out. The here and now sucked. "Do you think I could put on some clothes before you handcuff me and take me in? I knew it was too good to be true when they told me it was all over and no charges would be pressed."

"Oh for Pete's sake, cut the melodrama. I'm not here to arrest you. If I was, I'd have done that before…uh, you know," she said, her lovely girl-next-door face washed in a delicate blush.

He turned around and leaned against the wall, crossing his arms over his chest. "Before you screwed me?" He was deliberately insulting. "I thought maybe it was a new police procedure. Screw 'em and book 'em."

"There's no need to sulk. I wasn't exactly holding a gun to your head."

"I suppose I should be grateful since you definitely could have. But I'll have to tell you, babe, a loaded weapon—make it good or I'll blow your balls off—now *that* could give a guy a helluva case of erectile dysfunction. But if you're not here to arrest me, what is this about?"

"Why would you think I'm here to arrest you? What've you done?"

"Could you put the gun away?" Nick didn't like guns. AJ had a big collection, but they made

Nick's skin crawl. He was definitely a lover, not a fighter.

"Not until I know why you think I'd be here to arrest you. In fact, I'd be more comfortable if you'd move to the table and take a seat next to Sheila. I'd hate to have to shoot you in the butt if you tried to run out the door."

"Would you really shoot me in the butt?"

"Nah."

He was relieved. Not that he planned to run. He wanted answers. He was just checking.

"I'd aim for your leg or something. Your butt looks too good to shoot up." She laughed. "Sorry, cop humor." At his humorless look, she added, "I understand you're upset. You have every right to be. Let's both get dressed and I'll fill you in."

Okay. Curiosity definitely dispelled some of his anger. He pulled on his underwear and his slacks, then shrugged into his shirt but left it hanging open. Not knowing if this would be his last opportunity to see her naked, he unabashedly watched her dress.

"I know a sex therapist who could help you with your nudity issues. Never mind—that was you." Okay, maybe he was still a little pissed that she'd lied to him.

"You need to get over it." She pulled the black dress over her head, which left her looking just as sexy as she had looked naked. Her hair was tousled and the dress fit her like a second skin. "What are you pissed about? You're a guy who obviously wanted sex. You got what you wanted." She tugged it down over her thighs. "So, I'm not a sex therapist. It was still sex, and it was good sex, so could you give it a break?" She leaned against the wall he'd recently vacated. "Why don't you lose the attitude and take a seat and let's see if we can figure out what's going on?"

"Talk about attitude. That dominatrix thing wasn't much of a stretch for you, was it? You like to order people around."

"I'm used to people doing what I tell them to do. But then again, a gun goes a long way toward encouraging cooperation." She smiled with deceptive sweetness.

He sat in the chair across from Sheila and crossed his arms over his chest. "Your persuasive skills could use a little work."

"Really? I've never had that complaint before. Now why do you think I would arrest you?"

It had been his experience, from his embezzlement episode, that cops liked to mess with your head, but if she was asking what he'd done, maybe it didn't have anything to do with the embezzlement. "The money I embezzled. I paid it back and Gleeson agreed not to press charges, but it seemed too good to be true that that was the end of it."

He saw the light go on in her head. "That's why you looked familiar, not because you resembled that lousy picture but because you were on the tabloids in the grocery store. You embezzled half a million bucks and your brother's the nice guy who went on those reality shows to win it back for you."

It wasn't a pretty picture she'd just painted— he was a loser and Rourke was a hero. He bowed forward from the waist. "At your service. And if you're not here to arrest me, perhaps you could fill me in on what's going on. And exactly what lousy picture do I resemble or not resemble?"

She put away her gun and pulled out her badge, flashing it at him. "I'm Detective Serena Riggs with the BPD, precinct one-five-one. I've been working a money-laundering case for three months. The primary suspect is Nick Malone, a thirty-year-old, Caucasian male, approximately six feet one inches, one hundred eighty to one ninety-five pounds, dark hair, blue eyes." Damn. She could've been describing him. This did not sound good. "We received a tip that Nick Malone, also known as Slick Nick, would be arriving at this hotel yesterday."

In fact, this sounded like deep shit to him. Nick nodded. "So, that's why you bought me a beer in the bar?"

"Yeah. You definitely fit the description and Slick Nick has been known to use an alias or two."

Great. So, he'd been correct when he thought something was up with him being sent here to twiddle his thumbs. The sons of bitches were setting him up. Dammit. He'd landed in deep shit and he had a feeling he didn't know just how deep. But being set up for money laundering, that was pretty damn deep. And in the midst of realizing that his life was swirling down the toilet in some macabre Tidy Bowl dance, it occurred to his damaged ego that she hadn't been attracted to him, she'd been looking for her bad guy.

And speaking of bad guys, how did she know that he wasn't?

"How can you be sure I'm not Slick Nick using an alias? Maybe this is just a trap." He shook his head. Dammit, what was she thinking? She could have been putting herself in real danger.

She shook her head. "No trap. I'm positive you're not Slick Nick."

How could she be so sure? He raised his brow in question.

"Our source gave us means of positively identifying Nick Malone. Nick Malone is into bondage and spanking. But even more telling, he has a 'MOM' tattoo on his right butt cheek," she paused, a wicked glint of amusement dancing in her eyes, "and our source says he has a small penis. You don't have a tattoo and there's no way you could ever be considered small."

Things were looking up. He was in a mess, but she knew for sure he wasn't this Slick Nick character. And it was always nice to hear from a woman you'd just made love to that she didn't think you were operating with substandard equipment.

"Thanks. I think. So, you came here undercover looking for this guy Slick Nick, but you found me instead because those bastards set me up."

"It looks that way to me."

"And that's why you wanted me to take my pants off and turn around?" Geez, this part wasn't doing much for his ego.

She tried to look apologetic and failed miserably, betrayed by the glint of laughter in her eyes. "I had to get a positive ID one way or another."

"But you stayed when you knew I wasn't the man you're looking for…and you came back tonight."

She took a deep breath and looked him square in the eye. "I don't believe in coincidence. If it hadn't been for the tattoo—and the other thing—I would've been convinced you were Nick Malone. That's just too coincidental."

"Yeah. It does seem odd. I've been trying to figure out exactly what the company wanted me to do here. I guess I know now."

"When were you told you'd be coming here?"

"It was last-minute. They contacted me on Wednesday."

Serena nodded. "Our source met with our people on…" She thought for a moment. "It was a Tuesday."

Nick added two and two and came up with four. "Does this seem like a setup to you?"

"It looks that way to me."

"But how would they know?"

For one brief moment, pain lurked in her caramel-flecked eyes. "I think someone in my department is feeding Nick Malone information. I've been on his trail for three months. I'm good at what I do, but he's always one step ahead of me. I think there's a rat in my department."

"I'd say the shit just got a whole lot deeper." Getting set up for money laundering was no walk in the park, but discovering a rogue cop really upped the stakes.

Serena nodded and he saw a flicker of approval in her eyes. "I'm glad you understand what we're dealing with here. Talking to the wrong person in my department could get one of us or both of us killed. The only real lead I had was you and why you were here and who sent you. So, I came back tonight."

"And where does the sex fit in? Did you sleep with me so I'd cooperate with you?"

She looked at him as if he needed his head examined. "No. I slept with you because I wanted to. You're hot and we seem to have a mutual attraction going on."

She thought he was hot and that's why she'd slept with him. Any lingering hostility flew out the window. He admitted it. He was a soft sell. "That's the best news I've had all day and I'd really like to explore that mutual attraction, but expending a few brain cells to avoid doing jail time or becoming fish bait seems like a good idea. We need a plan, or do you already have one?"

"I think the best place to start is how you fit in and trace it back from there."

"How are you so sure I'm not involved? How do I know you aren't involved and this is just part of an elaborate setup?"

"You don't. You're in the same boat I am. You have to go with your gut and trust your instincts. If you want me to walk out that door and you can go about your merry way, that's the way we'll play it. If you want to check me out at the 151st to see if I'm legit, I'll pray for both our sakes you don't pick the wrong person to talk to, because I know all the guys there and even I don't know who I can trust at this point. Either one of those choices stands a good chance of landing you in prison or dead. And they don't bode too well for me either. I've gone out on a limb here and squared with you on what I know, but I can't make you trust me or work with me."

"It all sounds a little crazy, but it also ties into enough things that have made me wonder…"

Her look was sharp and enquiring, and he thought that she'd be formidable in an interrogation. "What kinds of things?"

"I have to backtrack a little."

"Take your time. I'm going to take notes. It helps later to go back and look at something that perhaps didn't jump out at me before. Detective work is mostly like bits of a puzzle and you simply have to find the missing pieces." She reached into her purse and pulled out a notebook and pen.

"A year ago, in a serious lapse of judgment, I embezzled half a million dollars from my employer." He shrugged, not particularly wanting to discuss it, as it hadn't been one of his finer moments. "I was smart enough to do it, not smart enough not to get caught."

"Most criminals aren't smart enough not to get caught."

"My employer agreed not to press charges as long as he got his money back with interest. I hadn't spent the money so that wasn't particularly a problem. Coming up with the interest was a big problem."

She nodded. "Your brother and the reality shows."

"Yep. Needless to say I didn't have a job. And at that point, since the whole world knew about what I'd done, I doubted I'd ever find another decent job. I figured I'd be lucky to land a position cleaning toilets at Fenway Park."

He hadn't been looking for sympathy, which was just as well because she sure didn't offer it. "Reasonable thought process. So how'd you get this position?"

"A friend of a friend of a friend knew of an opening. I went to the interview and they hired me."

"Did your background come up at the time? How did you handle that?"

"Of course it did. We discussed it. Harv Godfrey, the guy who hired me, told me that they realized everyone made mistakes because we were all human and they weren't worried about taking a chance on me."

"What'd you think about that? Didn't that seem like a very understanding attitude for them to take? The economy's not exactly booming. There's a huge labor pool out there. Why would they take a chance on you?"

Great! She made it sound as if he was the last of the genuine idiots not to have been suspicious. He was going to sound like even more of an idiot when he told her the truth. "I was desperate to get back on my feet."

"What were you hired to do? Who do you report to? What are your responsibilities?"

"I'm a salesman for them. I report to Harv. And my sole responsibility is sales. Mack Enterprises supplies the leads and they have another support division. I just talk the folks into it." He laughed, but it wasn't because he was amused. "I even called Harv today to tell him there was no need for me to be here. It didn't feel right to me. They've given me way too much leeway, but I didn't know what to do about my suspicions." He sighed. "Now, I've got a few questions of my own. How long have you been a cop? How many similar cases have you worked? Is all of your work undercover? Are you currently dating anyone?"

"I've been a cop for nine years, a detective for the last two. I've worked a couple of similar cases and my conviction rate is darn good. I put the bad guys in jail. My work involves undercover, but it's not the deep undercover you find in some departments." She slanted him an exasperated, reprimanding look. "And no, I'm not currently dating anyone, otherwise I wouldn't have jumped into bed with you."

That was a spot of bad news—not that she didn't have a boyfriend, just that he was so glad to hear it. The detail that had niggled at him earlier suddenly clicked. "Another thing I want to clear up. You weren't coming into my room last night, when I caught you at the door, were you?"

She didn't look away from him, but something flickered across her face. She was good, but so was he. "Why do you think that?"

"I didn't start to put it together until tonight, but last night the sound of the lock woke me up. I should have seen the light from the hall when you opened the door, but I never did. That's because you were already here, weren't you?" Something else clicked into place, another minor detail that he'd overlooked previously. "And you called the lovely Sheila by name. But I never mentioned her name after I found you in the room. So, if we're going to be square with one another, as you put it, why don't you tell me exactly when you came into my room?"

She shrugged. "I sent you the beer as a stall tactic. I didn't expect you to come back to your room so soon."

"So you were already here when I came back from the bar?"

She maintained her direct gaze and composure,

but the tense set of her shoulders betrayed her. "Yes."

Another piece of the puzzle slipped into place. "I thought I smelled your perfume when I came in, but I thought that was just because you were on my mind. You had to be in the closet. The only other place to hide in this room would've been the shower and I know for sure you weren't in there."

"Yes. I was just about to leave when I heard you at the door, so I ducked into the closet."

The shower. He'd been tied up in knots and hard as a rock for her when he'd returned to the room. Christ. She knew Sheila's name because she'd overheard him talking to Sheila about her. She'd listened to him jerk off in the shower to the image of her in his head.

"You heard, didn't you? You heard it all?" He felt like a thirteen-year-old who'd just been caught peering into the girls' locker room.

"Yes."

Jesus, this was mortifying. It was running a close second to being caught out for embezzlement. Actually, maybe it was more embarrassing. The embezzlement wasn't as personal, as revealing. "That was private."

"I know. I apologize. I really didn't mean to spy on you."

"How about you give me a break? You didn't mean to spy on me? You broke into my room."

"Yeah, but I never meant for you to show up here before I got out and back to the bar."

He knew it was inane, but he had to ask. "Why didn't you say something?"

"Because I kept thinking I'd get a look at your butt. I just needed to ID you with the tattoo."

He gathered his courage. Might as well find out the absolute depths of his humiliation. "Were you laughing at the poor slob you had so ratcheted up or were you totally disgusted?" Damn. Plastered across the tabloids was nothing compared to masturbating while the woman who inspired you listened.

She raised her chin a notch and even though color stained her face, she met his gaze straight on. "I certainly wasn't laughing and any disgust I felt was with myself, because I thought it was really hot and you turned me on."

He blinked and stood. "You heard me tell Sheila that you turned me on, that I thought you had great legs and in those boots…"

That look was back in her eyes. "I believe the term was dick-hardening."

"I believe you're right." He took a step toward her. "How did that make you feel?"

"Hot and bothered."

"Let me guess. You didn't want to feel hot and bothered."

"Not particularly. I thought you were into light S&M and I didn't know what you'd done with Sheila, or what you were planning to do."

Thanks. He'd had his quota of humiliation for the day. He couldn't move the topic along fast enough. "So, back to our plan. My guess is the deal was going to go down the last day Slick Nick was here, but that's been changed now. I don't think you're supposed to catch me now. I'm just being moved into place. This is all preliminary setup," Nick said.

Serena nodded. "It sounds reasonable. The important thing is not to raise any red flags. The worst thing we could do would be to tip our hand."

She was totally oblivious to how sexy she was. However, he was aware enough for both of them. He was also aware of the seriousness of the situation. "If we're right, and I think we are, and whoever is behind this has the slightest inkling we're onto them, we'll both disappear?"

"That's my take. The way I see it, there are three options. One, I can report back that I couldn't get a look at your butt, which really doesn't work well for either one of us. Since it would seem I'd tried and failed, twice, then I couldn't logically continue to pursue you. Option two is that I report you have a tattoo."

Nausea rose inside him and he stopped her, shaking his head. "Nope. No way. I'm not getting tattooed. I have a thing about needles. Not going to happen." No one really liked needles, but he had a serious phobia about them. It'd made going to the doctor as a kid a real picnic.

The sympathetic look she shot him surprised him. She was a cop who risked being shot at on a regular basis. "No, I never meant you'd actually have to get a tattoo—I would just tell them that. But the idea's not particularly feasible anyway. It'd probably raise their suspicions and they'd figure out I'm bluffing."

Nick felt better that she'd shelved it as soon as she'd thrown it out there. And he was relieved she hadn't laughed at him. Needles were to him what snakes or heights or enclosed spaces were to some other people. "And what's behind door number three?"

"It's the one I feel has the most potential. I report that your bare derriere is, in fact, tattoo free."

"Okay. I'm sensing a *but* here, no pun intended. Otherwise it's the same as option one."

She tilted her head to one side. "Well, here's the difference. I tell them that although you didn't have a tattoo, you were very much into being dominated and spanked. I could say that, in my professional opinion, the tattoo Debi Majette mentioned was likely a temporary one. I'm fully convinced you're our man and I've got the situation firmly in control."

If she said so. "Okay…."

"Because you liked the domination game so much and it didn't work out with your new girlfriend, I'm your new dom and you're my love slave."

"You don't think they'll be suspicious?"

"I've discovered two universal truths since I've been involved in police work. The first is criminals are stupid and careless." Nick laughed. "What? If they weren't, the jails wouldn't be so full, would they?"

She definitely saw things in black and white, no shades of gray blurred in between. And certainly, if he'd been as smart as he thought he was, he wouldn't have got caught. "But you've also said you don't believe in coincidence and wouldn't it seem like a huge coincidence to them if I was into S&M just like Nick Malone?"

She shook her head. "When I was researching the whole light bondage thing, well, there are more people out there who are into that than you might think. And there's also the fact that bad cops are arrogant. It takes a certain measure of arrogance to move outside the law you've sworn to uphold in the first place. So, whoever this is already considers himself smarter than me and you and the rest of the guys in the precinct. You can be certain he considers himself smarter than Slick Nick Malone. He'll definitely underestimate us."

It was so far out there, it made a weird sort of sense. "I suppose it could work."

"It could definitely work. It has to work. It's the only recourse that has a real chance."

"Do you move in with me?"

"No. The way it works in domination-ville is you clean my house, run my errands and then you do whatever makes me happy sexually. You won't actually move in, but you will need to spend a good bit of time there. You'll also have to run a certain number of my errands, because I'm sure we'll be watched, but you don't have to clean my apartment. Although, for this to really work, you've got to get your head into it. Think of it as method acting."

"Is that what you do when you go undercover?"

"Exactly."

For about a second he toyed with asking her if she'd been acting when they'd made love, but instinctively he knew better. He'd felt the same fierce want driving her that had ripped through him.

"I can do that."

"You've got to be sure. Bad cops are arrogant, but they're not stupid. Whoever he is, he'll be watching and if we slip up or something doesn't seem right, he'll be on to us." She stood and suddenly she was, once again, the dominatrix from last night. "But the real relationship between the dominatrix and the slave is absolute devotion. The slave is at the total beck and call of the dom. Day or night. It's whatever I want you to do, whenever I want you to and however I want you to. It's all about sex and power and control. Do you think you can handle that?"

"One last question."

"Sure."

"You'll report that you believe the tattoo was temporary…"

"Yeah. That's not so farfetched."

"But does that mean you have to tell them I have a little dick?"

"'Fraid so, tiger. I'll tell them it doesn't require a magnifier, but I'll have to put out the word that you underwear shop in the boys' department."

"Ouch."

"I know that hurts. How about I kiss it and make it all better?"

9

"YOU LUCKED OUT, MALONE."

Nick held the cell phone to his ear but didn't respond immediately, checking the fit of his suit jacket in the mirror. Nice. Very nice. Let the cop wait on him. "How's that? Did you just discover you have a tumor?"

"Very funny, douche bag. Your stooge is a freak show, same as you. Seems you're not the only one into the whips, chains and bootlicking."

"What?" Nick stepped away from and turned his back on Bennie, his regular tailor, who'd been pinning up the cuffs on his pants.

"Yeah, the cop handling the case went in as a dominatrix based on what your ex had to say. Apparently your fall boy was fond of the whip she took with her and her red stiletto heels."

"What about the tattoo?"

"She's sure it must've been a temporary one. It's the only thing that doesn't fit on this guy. Looks like you've pulled it off, Nicky. She's convinced he's her man and she's going to keep him under close surveillance. Now this is the part that's going to hurt you. She's got him set up as her slave. I heard she was going out today to buy him a collar to wear when he's at her place. She's tough as nails, Nicky, and I'm sure she can spank nice and hard."

Nick knew this cop would say anything to get a rise out of him. The problem was, he was lonely. Unless she got paid for it, finding a woman to fulfill his particular needs wasn't all that easy. Especially when it was important for him to keep a low profile. Jealousy arced through him that O'Malley was enjoying what he missed. If the cop wasn't just playing with his mind. "She really thinks O'Malley's me? She's really set up as his dom?" He couldn't keep the note of wistfulness out of his voice.

"Gives you a hard-on just thinking about it, doesn't it?" The hateful laugh on the other end of the phone line grated on Nick's raw nerves, especially because the cop was right. "Yeah. I'd say a week, two at the most, and you can transfer the files and send O'Malley in to pick up the money, not that he'll know what he's doing. We'll nab him when he does the pickup, he'll take your fall and, if you're careful, that will be the end of that."

"I'll let Jo-Jo know. He hasn't been happy about the development. Let's plan for a week. The sooner it goes down the better. Call me back tomorrow and I'll confirm the time frame."

He pressed the end button, hanging up on the cop who'd saved his ass but whom Nick despised.

Within a couple of weeks, the heat should be off of him. Nick O'Malley would rot in jail for a long time on his behalf, but he didn't feel guilty. Hey, if the guy was stupid, he deserved what he got—survival of the fittest.

He returned to where Bennie waited patiently in front of the triple mirror.

Still, he couldn't shake his resentment over O'Malley getting that kind of action while he, Nick, went without.

"PAY UP," AJ said, before Nick had a chance to open his mouth.

Nick slid onto the stool across from AJ, between Matt and Tim. Dougal's was crowded and noisier than usual this evening. It must be the televised fight scheduled for later tonight. "What makes you think you won't be paying me?" He had the cash in his pocket but he had no intention of rolling over for AJ.

AJ leveled a knowing look his way. "Because for a guy who's addicted to women, you look way too relaxed to have been without one for thirty days."

Tim poured Nick a beer from the communal pitcher.

Nick hoisted his mug at AJ in mocking salute. "Yeah, I suppose I don't look like you."

Tim and Matt laughed and even AJ grinned. Nick sipped from the mug and put it back onto the table. He pulled five crisp Benjamin Franklins out of his pocket and tossed them on the table. "You win."

Matt grunted in disgust. "Man, are you for real? After you passed up all those other women, I laid odds you'd make it."

"How close did you come to going the distance?" Tim asked.

Nick took another swallow of cold brew and shrugged. "Twenty-nine days."

"Twenty-four lousy hours and you couldn't make it? Man, that's pathetic." Matt dug in his jeans' pocket, pulled out a twenty and threw it on top of the pay-up cash.

"Actually, it was less than twenty-four hours. It was more along the lines of nineteen and some odd minutes." Nick set the record straight, although he felt sort of bad about Matt losing twenty bucks on him.

AJ scooped up the bills and tucked them in his pocket. "At least you're not whining about the dough," he said to Nick.

"Are you kidding? It's the best five hundred bucks I ever spent. This woman is really special." He'd said it to jam on the guys, but he realized with a start it was true.

"I think our boy might've been bitten by the love bug," AJ said.

Good deal. That was exactly what he and Serena wanted his friends and family to think. Only Nick and Serena would know the truth. Nick had thought about confiding in his brother, Rourke, and then decided against it. All their lives, Rourke had been the responsible one. All their lives Rourke had bailed Nick out of "situations." It was time for Nick to step up to the plate and handle his own life. Plus, keeping his friends and family in the dark meant keeping them safe.

He didn't have to fabricate a goofy smile. He just thought about going over to Serena's place after this. "She's incredible." It wasn't just her hot legs and the great sex. She was tough and funny and smart and he sensed a sweet vulnerability as well.

"Damn, Skippy. You just donated five hundred bucks to me and you've got a stupid smile on your face. You're worrying me," AJ said.

"Man's got a point," Tim agreed, reaching past the pitcher and snagging a tortilla chip.

"She's different from anyone I've ever met before," Nick said. He'd never realized how hot it was to have a naked woman handling a gun with a look on her face that said, though she'd rather not, she wouldn't hesitate to blow off a ball or two if necessary.

"Hey, maybe it's Sheila," Matt said, still bent out of shape over his twenty. "She's definitely different."

Nick grinned. "She's met Sheila. I think Sheila was jealous."

"What's her name?" Tim asked. "How'd you meet her?"

"Her name's Serena and we met at the hotel

bar." He didn't want to lie to his friends, but these guys were definitely getting the sanitized version. And he had *met* her, after a fashion, when he was having his burger. He checked his watch. "Listen, I've got to go. I'm supposed to be at her place in half an hour. She's making dinner."

"Man, three days and this chick's already got you whipped. You ought to stay and watch the game with us, just to show her she doesn't own you. I'll even buy dinner." AJ grinned. "I just came into some money."

Nick shook his head. Right. Like he'd take advice from AJ. "Let's see, sit around with you guys or spend time with one very hot woman? Wow, that's a tough decision." Nick pushed away from the table and stood. "Catch you guys later."

"Hold on a sec. Some vital statistics would be nice. What color hair? Nice bod? I want to take notes on what was worth half a grand."

"About five-eight. Dirty blond. Cute nose with freckles. Nice legs. Pretty much nice everything."

"Big tits?" Matt had a thing for big tatas.

AJ should introduce Candy to Matt. Matt would like her beer bottle trick. "She's not pitching forward when she walks, but everything's nicely proportioned."

"What does Serena do for a living?" Tim asked. Tim actually saw past women's *vital statistics*.

They'd decided to run with the cover she'd used when she introduced herself. AJ was going to have a freakin' kitten over this. "She's a sex therapist."

AJ closed his eyes for a brief moment. "You know, you really do suck."

That alone was worth the five hundred bucks he'd just forked out.

SERENA CHECKED the oven timer—another twenty minutes—and finished washing the dishes she'd used to prepare dinner. She told herself it was ridiculous to be nervous that O'Malley would be showing up at any minute.

She'd dressed the dominatrix part, but she'd never role-played at home. It had always been a work thing. It was much harder to get her head into playing a role when she was in her own space.

A knock sounded at her door and butterflies took flight in her stomach. She gave the counter one last swipe and hung the dish towel on the hook. She double-checked through the peephole. O'Malley. She threw the lock and opened the door.

"Come in." She'd forgotten just how blue his eyes were, especially in contrast to the sweep of dark lashes. She'd also forgotten the bone-melting effect of his smile.

"These are for you." He held out a bouquet of mixed blossoms, the kind offered in the produce section at the market. Some detective she was. She'd been so busy mooning over him she hadn't even noticed them in his hand. "I hope you're not allergic or anything."

She took the flowers from him, her fingers brushing his, the blooms' perfume mingling with his scent. Those butterflies returned to her belly in full flight.

"No. I'm not allergic. Thanks. Come on in and I'll put them in water." She needed to check her calendar. She must be hormonal. That would explain the crushing sentimentality she felt over Nick's bouquet. "They're very nice but you know you didn't have to do this. Love slaves aren't required to arrive bearing flowers."

Nick smiled at her joke and offered a half-shouldered shrug. "I'm lost when it comes to love slave protocol." He closed the door behind him. "Besides I brought them because I wanted you to have them."

He tilted her chin up with one finger and pressed a brief kiss to the corner of her mouth, not staying long enough for her to kiss him back. It wasn't the hot, frantic I-want-to-tear-your-panties-off kind of kiss from yesterday. This was tender and sweet, and a different kind of heat flushed her.

Between the kiss and the fact that he'd brought her flowers because he wanted her to have them, she floundered as if a strong gust of unexpected wind had blown her off course.

"You don't have any idea, do you?" he asked, his voice low and quiet.

"Any idea about what?" If he was going to turn around now and make some crappy comment about her not knowing what to do with these flowers, she'd dump them on his head.

"You really don't know how beautiful you are, do you?"

Not what she'd expected to hear. At all. It could've been any line from a barfly. Except O'Malley wasn't a barfly and it made her feel touched and vulnerable, and in a panic she lashed out.

"You know, this isn't necessary. I don't need to be seduced with the flowers and the pretty words."

Hurt, anger, embarrassment flashed across his face. "Good. I think you already took care of the seduction. It was an observation."

She sounded like a bitch. "I'm sorry. That was a crappy thing for me to say."

"Yeah, it was." Some men would've sulked all evening but O'Malley just looked at her as if he knew what was going on in her head and that stirred up another frightfest for her altogether.

Unfortunately, she couldn't let it go. "I'm nothing special."

"I'm entitled to my opinion and I'll beg to differ with you on that one."

"Listen, O'Malley. I do undercover work. It's my job to become someone I'm not. I assume a role and play whatever part's required. I can pass for a lot of things, but when you take away all of the disguises, I'm not a sophisticated business woman, I'm not a hooker, I'm not a bag lady and I'm not a dominatrix. I'm just plain me, a poor girl from the wrong side of Cleveland."

He stared her down. Hard. "They need water."

"Water. Right. This way," she said, getting herself together. She gestured toward the fishbowl on the plant shelf that separated the entryway from the den. "Meet Sucka and Mutha. They may look mismatched but it's a very symbiotic relationship."

"Ah, the greeting committee." Actually, that was exactly why she had them there, so she walked in and saw them and knew her apartment wasn't empty. O'Malley smiled and bent down to peer into the bowl, putting him eye-to-eye with Sucka. "Nice to meet you."

He straightened and glanced around her apartment, clearly curious. It was clean, neat and comfortable enough, but... She'd bet a dollar to a donut all of O'Malley's women possessed stylish decorating senses and cute little dogs or cuddly kitties. Which really didn't matter either way. Serena wasn't a Barbie girl and she sure as heck didn't live in a Barbie world.

"Vintage Goodwill and Salvation Army," she said with a sweep of her hand, as she moved through the space that doubled as dining room and den. "I don't like to shop. Plus I'd rather save for a house and fill it with castaway furniture than continue to rent an apartment and furnish it with new, expensive things."

Nick smiled. "You sound like my brother, Rourke. You'd like Rourke. He's a great guy."

Serena nodded. "I actually saw him once on that second reality show he did—someone had it

on a TV at the station. He seemed nice enough."
He did seem nice enough, but he'd come across
as a bit insipid. "But he didn't seem to have
your…I don't know…personality…sparkle."

For a split second he looked startled and then
a smile spread from his mouth to his eyes. "Thank
you, Serena Riggs."

"You're welcome, Nick O'Malley."

Nick followed her into the kitchen and she
knew a moment of silent embarrassment. No one
had ever brought her flowers before. She didn't
own a vase. She opened the cabinet. A large jar sat
on the top shelf. She stood on tiptoe and reached
for it. She couldn't quite get it. O'Malley came up
behind her.

"Here. Let me." He reached around her, trapping her between his big body and the counter. He
smelled even better than she remembered. His
chest was a solid wall behind her; his breath teased
her hair. He braced one hand on her shoulder, his
fingers branding her through her clothes, while he
reached with the other hand. "Is this the one?"

He could probably hear how stinking loud her
heart was thumping. "Yes." He handed her the jar
and stepped away. "Thanks."

"Something smells great," he said, leaning
against the counter, his blue eyes watchful.

"It's chicken potpie." She filled the jar with
water and put the flowers in.

"Hold on a second." He took the flower-filled
jar from her. "Do you have a pair of scissors?"

What was he up to? "Sure." She handed him a pair from the junk drawer.

He pulled the flowers out and laid them on the counter. "You forgot this." He opened a little plastic packet and dumped the white powder into the water. "The flowers will last longer that way." He trimmed the stems and returned them to the jar, taking a few seconds to arrange them a little more artfully than just shoving them in as she'd done.

"Much nicer. Thank you." For a second she thought about feeling inadequate that he'd known what to do and been so much better at arranging the flowers than she had, but she dismissed it. Thus far, flowers hadn't figured prominently in her life. She was still in control of the things that mattered.

An open doorway led from the kitchen back into the eating nook. She placed the flowers in the center of the table. Serena didn't like clutter and she didn't care for froufrou, but this worked. Even in the jar, they added an elegant touch to her simply set table. She turned around. Nick, his shoulder propped against the doorjamb, arms crossed in front of his chest, filled the doorway. "Very nice. Thanks, again."

"I'm glad you like them." His words were innocuous enough, but his gaze flicked over her from head to toe and a shiver chased down her spine.

The timer went off. "Dinner."

He straightened but still took up half the doorway. "Excuse me." She brushed past him. Her shoulder grazed his chest, her hip his thigh. Her body quickened at the brief contact.

She pulled the potpie out of the oven. Nick peered over her shoulder. "Oh, honey, that doesn't look like any chicken potpie I've ever heated up from the freezer."

She was pleased with the way it had turned out. Fragrant steam rose from the slits in the golden, flaky crust. She smiled. "Good food is my one extravagance."

"You like to cook and I like to eat. I think we could be on to something here. What can I do to help?"

"I'll serve the salad and you can put the plates on the table." She pulled the bowl out of the fridge, divvied the greens between two salad plates, and handed them off to Nick.

Working together, within a few minutes they were seated at the table enjoying salad, chicken potpie, and fresh asparagus with lemon and butter.

Serena quietly held her breath while Nick took his first bite of potpie.

"Oh, my God. This is one of the best things I've ever put in my mouth. Do you eat like this all the time?"

His enthusiasm pleased her. Cooking was a joy in her life. She loved all aspects of it: menu planning, shopping for the ingredients, the chopping, dicing, mixing, testing until she got it just the way she wanted it.

"Thanks. I do eat this way most of the time. Of course, it means I eat a lot of leftovers."

"Honey, it wouldn't be a hardship at all to eat this again. But I think with me at your table, you're not going to have any leftovers."

"That's fine. I don't mind the leftovers, but it's nice to have someone to eat with, especially someone who enjoys food." She didn't mind living alone, but she disliked dining alone.

"What's not to enjoy? How'd you get interested in cooking?"

"I've been interested since I can remember. I think I was born interested. I took over the cooking for my mother when I was so young I had to stand on a chair to reach the counter and the stove."

"Did she mind you taking over her kitchen?"

"No. She was always really busy. I think she was just glad to have me take care of it."

"No kidding. People would pay for this." He pointed at his plate with his fork. "*I* would pay for this."

"That's very flattering. If I hadn't been a cop, I would've probably tried my hand at being a chef." She wasn't sure where that had come from. Maybe it was because O'Malley was so easy to talk to. Perhaps it was his enthusiasm over her hobby. Regardless, she'd just shared with him what she'd never mentioned to another soul. If he laughed at the idea she supposed she'd learn to keep her mouth shut.

He didn't laugh. "It's obviously a passion, so why'd you choose a badge and a gun instead of a whisk and a pastry brush? Seems a lot safer if the only thing you have to worry about is whether your soufflé falls instead of if some wise guy invites you to check out the local landfill in a Dumpster." Was that curiosity or concern in his voice?

"Nah. They dump all the bodies in the harbor."

Nick simply looked at her. Oops. He had a sense of humor, but he didn't seem to find that very funny. "Sorry. Morbid cop humor."

A frown knit his brow. "And this is your chosen profession because…"

"Would you believe great pay and outstanding benefits?"

"No. Sorry. I do read the newspaper occasionally. You'll have to do better than that." When Nick fixed his blue eyes on her like that, it was as if the only thing that could possibly hold his interest was her answer.

"I became a cop because the bad guys belong off the streets. And up until I figured out someone in the department's sold us out, I thought I was surrounding myself with the good guys." Like a monk donning a horsehair shirt for penance, she decided to share her dirty secret. She smoothed the napkin in her lap. "My father was in jail the day my mother brought me home from the hospital. I was two before he was released. By my third birthday, he was back in prison. It's proven to be something of a pattern for him."

"That must've been a tough way to grow up." Nick said, matter-of-factly with a touch of sympathy.

Serena shrugged. "It was what it was. I don't think criminals stop to think about how their actions affect the people who care about them. The worst part has always been that instead of taking responsibility for his actions, he's always said he was doing it to better our family." She gave an inelegant snort. "Right."

"That's messed up."

"Tell me about it. According to Dad, every job he pulled, every scam, was just trying to make a little money to take care of his family."

"I'm not sensing a great affection."

She despised him. It hadn't always been that way. She'd adored the father who'd shown up periodically in her life, each time promising a fresh new start, that things were going to be different now for him and his girls. And she'd believed him time after time until she'd finally begun to realize that his promise of not having to move from one roach-infested apartment to another, of a small house they could call their own, was just a bill of goods he was selling. Love, trust and adoration had eroded to a sense of betrayal, which had then turned into something all the more powerful: hate. Her mother referred to her father as a dreamer. Serena had come to regard him as a con artist. "No, there's no affection."

"What about your mother? Are you close?"

"We stay in touch. She's the exact opposite of my father. She's always worked at least two, sometimes three, jobs to keep a roof over our heads and food on the table. And she lets him come back every time he gets out." She shook her head.

"You think she's foolish?" Nick placed his napkin on the table, next to his plate.

"Of course. Don't you?"

"She sounds like an optimist. Maybe she thinks he'll change. Come out rehabilitated."

"The recidivism rate staggers the mind and blows that theory out of the water. It's like a dog, once he bites, you can never trust him not to bite again. And my father will never change."

Nick wasn't exactly comfortable with the way the conversation was going, but this wasn't about him—it was about Serena and her family.

"When's the last time you saw them?"

"It's been a while," she said. He just looked at her, patiently, expectantly. She squirmed in her chair. "What? Okay, so I haven't been back since I left. Eleven years. I haven't…I couldn't…" She stumbled, feeling compelled to explain to Nick what she'd never perhaps acknowledged to herself. "When I left, it was like breaking free from shackles. I was no longer defined by who my father was and the choices he made."

Nick traced a line along the condensation on his water glass. He considered her, his head tilted to one side. "Have you ever thought that maybe you became a cop to get back at your father?"

The truth slapped her in the face. "I never thought of it that way."

"Well, if you ever decide to get out of police work, you should pursue the cooking gig. It might be mentally healthier to spend your time and energy creating something instead of trying to destroy something…or someone."

He made her sound like a monster. "I'm good at what I do."

"You seem to be. You also seem to be a bright, determined woman. You'd be good at whatever you set your mind to. I think it's more important to ask yourself if what you do is good for you."

10

"YOU KNOW YOU DON'T have to do that," Serena said.

Nick rinsed the silverware and placed it in the drain. "You cooked. I ate. Now that means I wash. It's only fair. I consider myself lucky you're not going to make me scrub your toilet with a toothbrush."

She laughed, the light catching shades of gold in her hair, and picked up a dishtowel to dry. "Where'd you come up with that?"

"I did some Internet surfing on the domination thing. I'll probably get spammed to death now, but I thought I should know a little bit more about it so that I don't say or do something stupid that might jeopardize our cover."

"What'd you think?" She stretched to put the glasses on the second shelf and Nick stood with his hands in the dishwater, totally distracted by the way her skirt rode up the back of her thigh, leaving a long, luscious expanse of leg open to his viewing.

He'd sort of hoped for blue jeans and a T-shirt.

Not that he was complaining about the short skirt and stiletto heels. But he knew it was a costume. He knew in his gut it wasn't something the true Serena Riggs would wear and he'd hoped for more of a glimpse of the real woman behind the role. He knew the other outfits were also costumes, props for the role she was playing. This was hot, but in his gut he knew jeans and a T-shirt would've been hotter, because it would've been her.

She turned to face him. "Hello?"

"Just admiring how organized your cabinets are," he said with a smirk.

"A lech, a slacker, and I think you're lying too. Do I need to get my whip?"

"Better that than the clothespins." He'd seen photos of guys with clothespins clipped to their equipment, in fact it had taken him a couple of seconds to figure out that what resembled a freaky undernourished porcupine was the guy's equipment. His first thought had been *ouch*. His second thought, *no freaking way*. "But I'm getting back to work now." He washed a plate.

"You have done your research." She didn't crack a smile. "You're safe. I'm fresh out of clothespins. But I could maybe round up a twist tie or two."

He shuddered, considering which of his body parts might accommodate a twist tie. "I don't even want to know."

She grinned and it was so cute he almost dropped the bowl he was washing. "I just made that up."

"Paybacks are hell."

She sobered. "Speaking of paybacks, I've been thinking about Malone and where to go with this. Have you ever seen a guy that might look like you? Or has anyone in the company ever mentioned it?"

"No. But we need to get something straight right from jump street. I'm not going to just stand around while you handle this."

"Oh course not. You're an important part of my cover."

He could tell, she wasn't getting it. "Partners. Fifty-fifty."

"I don't do partners. Well, not since I was in patrol. As a detective, I've always worked alone."

"It's a new day. Partners or nothing."

She narrowed her eyes at him. "Don't be stupid. You could get yourself killed out there alone."

"Yeah, so could you. You need me and I need you, but we do it together. This is the deal, no one's bailing my ass out of the sling this time except me."

She stared at him. "You're really not in a position to negotiate."

"Neither are you, sweetheart. And just think of all the insight I can give you into the criminal mind." She hesitated and he pressed the issue. "This is a deal breaker."

"Okay. Fine. Partners."

He was underwhelmed by her graciousness, but all that really mattered was that she'd agreed. Without a doubt, it hadn't been easy for her.

"So I think the first thing we should do is go into the company's files and check it out."

"Go into? You wouldn't, by chance, be referring to hacking?"

Damn. He thought she might be picky on this particular point. "Don't get hung up on semantics. Just hear me out, okay?"

She crossed her arms over her chest. "Okay."

"So, we go into the company files—"

"Let me guess. You know how to do this."

"Well, yeah. So, we get in and take a look. My guess is they have a couple of dummy corporations set up that should show up as a common factor along the way. Then they could roll the money through."

"You sound pretty sure of yourself."

"I'm guessing. But if I were setting it up I'd do it that way. Otherwise, it's too obvious, too traceable. It's less likely to raise a red flag. See what I mean?"

"It makes sense. What about firewalls? They wouldn't just leave their files vulnerable."

"We'll go around them."

"You're scary, O'Malley."

"Why? Because I'm so good?"

"No. Because you still think like a crook."

JO-JO SMILED and a chill chased down Nick Malone's back and grabbed him by the balls. Fear didn't produce the same high as a little bit of pain. And death didn't appeal to him at all.

"I got a good report from our friend today. He says the plan is working like a charm."

"Thank you for telling me, Jo-Jo. That's very good news. I'm happy." He almost breathed a sigh of relief. Nick had been worried Jo-Jo was going to ask him about his tattoo, which he hadn't yet had removed.

"I'm not happy. Do I look happy?"

Geez. How was he supposed to answer that? His palms began to sweat again. If he said Jo-Jo looked happy, he was calling him a liar. If he said Jo-Jo didn't look happy, it sounded as if he was criticizing him.

Jo-Jo waved a hand in disgust. "Forget it. Let's discuss instead the source of my displeasure. The plan is working like a charm, except for your left-over mess—Debi Majette. It's very sloppy work that she's still hanging around. People like Debi get to be a nuisance. You know what you do with a nuisance? You get rid of it. Then it don't bother you no more. I'm very unhappy that you leave a nuisance around me. However, I'm very fortunate that my friend is taking care of this nuisance for me. He shows me the proper respect."

Anger bubbled up inside Nick and threatened to overflow. That double-crossing bastard cop. "I told him I'd take care of Debi and he told me I was stupid." He almost kept his voice calm.

Jo-Jo shook his head. "Careful, Nick. You insult my friend, you insult me."

Nick bowed his head to keep the murder in his eyes from showing. "I apologize, Jo-Jo."

"That's better. You should thank our friend that Debi Majette won't be identifying anyone."

"Did he kill her?" Dammit. He'd wanted that pleasure for himself. The bitch had said he had a little dick.

"You have so much to learn." Jo-Jo shook his head. "Our friend can offer you an important lesson in finesse. It would be so crass to kill her. And losing the things one holds dear is so much more painful sometimes than dying yourself." Nick recalled with chilling clarity the day his father had died and how he'd felt knowing Jo-Jo was responsible. "Did you know Debi had a poodle she was very attached to? She misses him now. And Debi has family that she wants to take good care of by not indulging in any more indiscretions. Make sure you properly thank our friend for cleaning up your mess."

Sometimes Nick wondered if Jo-Jo was emotionally and mentally stable. That would, however, remain an eternal mystery 'cause asking wasn't worth Nick's life.

"I'll be sure to thank him." He'd take care of depositing the payoff money tomorrow.

"You do that. And watch yourself, Nicky." Jo-Jo smiled. "You don't want to become a nuisance."

SERENA WAS more relaxed now, more at ease. Maybe it was getting dinner out of the way, maybe it was coming up with a plan of attack or maybe she was getting used to having Nick here in her space, even though he'd bullied her into that partner thing.

Nick packed his laptop away and sat on the sofa, beside her.

"So, what did your friends have to say about you losing your bet?" she asked.

Nick shrugged and stretched his arm along the back of the sofa. Honestly, she could swear she felt his heat, even though he wasn't touching her. "AJ was five hundred bucks happier. Matt sulked because he lost twenty dollars on me."

She knew guys did that kind of stuff. Obviously he had more money to blow than she did. "How close were you to winning?"

He toyed with her hair, his fingers brushing her neck. Just that brief touch sent heat spiraling through her. "Less than twenty-four hours."

What? "I didn't know it was that close. My God. Five hundred dollars. I would've made you wait if I'd known."

"I'll tell you like I told them." He skimmed his fingers along her shoulder, his blue eyes holding hers, her breath catching somewhere in her chest. "It was worth every penny."

That set her heart racing. Had anyone ever made her feel so special? "Well. That's certainly a good answer. Insane, but good. What else did you tell them?"

"Trust me. They would've liked every lurid detail. But they didn't learn any. They did, however, specifically request your measurements."

She thought about the monster breasts on Sheila the blow-up doll. "I don't even want to know."

He didn't touch her, but his gaze caressed her breasts and then traveled down the length of her legs. "I told them you were perfectly proportioned."

"Hmmm." That tingling flush started between her legs and radiated. He could do that with just a look and a few well-chosen words. "Another good answer."

He checked his watch. "Isn't this the part of the evening when we play master and servant?" With a sly grin, he lowered his gaze in mock subservience. "Your pleasure is my pleasure."

"Hmmm. I like that—my pleasure is your pleasure. Let me think this through. You cleaned the kitchen. I gave you a grocery list and a couple of other errands for tomorrow. I believe you've earned the right to grovel at my feet."

"I did that groveling thing the first night we met, if you'll recall. I'm really hoping you're not going to ask me to lick your boots."

"Licking my boots seems like a waste, especially since I'm not even wearing them and, I'll be honest, I can think of things I'd much rather you lick than my boots. I might even find a couple of things I'd like to lick myself."

"I like the way your mind works."

"Wicked and warped?"

"It's a start. Where's your little riding crop?"

"It's still in my bag. Why? Do you want me to spank you?"

"No. I want you to get it and give it to me."

"Forget it. It's mine."

"Oh, honey, it's time for you to learn to share your toys."

"I don't want to share my toys."

"Come on, baby, we're partners and it's my turn."

"I never agreed to partners outside the case."

"Partners all the way."

"But I don't want to be spanked."

"That's good, because I don't want to spank you. Now bring me that whip and I promise we'll both be very happy in a very short period of time, partner."

"This isn't fair."

"What's not fair, baby? I need you to trust me."

"But…" She was hard-pressed to say exactly what wasn't fair about it, except that he wanted control of the situation. This wasn't just about sex. This was a test.

"If I do anything that you don't like or that makes you uncomfortable all you have to do is say, 'brake.' I promise. Trust me, honey."

Famous last words.

"And take your clothes off," he added.

"You first," she shot back. He didn't get to be totally in charge.

Nick laughed, low and wicked. "I thought you'd never ask. How about we do this together?"

The room separated them and she grew hotter still as they undressed for one another.

He was a totally spectacular man, hard in all the right places, some places harder than others. His gaze devoured her. "Now bring me that riding crop."

She retrieved the riding crop from her handbag. Creep. He knew how hard it was for her to relinquish control. He wanted control? She'd give him so much control his dick would fall off from being so hard.

She deliberately licked the shaft from the tasseled end to the hard, rounded handle. "Was this what you wanted?"

"Yes."

Fine. She'd already reduced him to a one-syllable response. She sank to the floor, on all fours, and put the quirt in her mouth, clenching it in her teeth.

"Oh," he said.

Ostensibly, she was giving up control, but she wasn't sure any longer that was the way it worked. Slowly, deliberately, excited by the sway of her own breasts and bottom, she crossed the room on her hands and knees.

She stopped in front of O'Malley and dropped the riding crop on the floor at his feet.

"Uh-uh. Pick it up and give it to me."

Dammit. She had his number. He was asking her to symbolically hand over the control.

Slanting him an evil glance, she picked up the leather whip and handed it to him. "There you are…master."

That happened to be the final thing that sent him over the edge. His flag pole sprang to full attention. Nick O'Malley had a thing or two to learn about who was in control. She raised herself up on her knees, she slid her hands along his hair-covered thighs, parting his knees. Bending forward, she dragged her tongue up his thick shaft, one long movement from the base to the glistening tip. Ahhh. She teased her tongue against the slitted opening and then swirled it around his knob. O'Malley groaned and sank against the couch.

She smiled to herself and took him into her mouth, her lips and her tongue paying homage to the length and breadth of his velvet-covered pole. She eased her lips along his shaft and swirled her tongue over the tight sacks at his root and then took them in her mouth, wrapping her fingers around his length as she suckled him gently in her mouth. His rod surged against her fingertips. She loved the taste of him in her mouth, his hot firmness in her hand.

"Enough." He stayed her with the single word.

She released him, but remained kneeling between his thighs.

He captured the striated leather ends of the riding crop in his mouth. Then, his blue gaze burning hot as a true flame, he reached out and teased the wet leather tips against her breasts, circling her mounds in smaller and smaller circles. Finally, when she was hot and wet and gasping he plied the tip against her distended nipple. And then the other one.

"Stand up," he said.

She stood and so did he.

"Kneel on the couch and face the back." She hesitated and he added, "Trust me."

She realized she'd never have gone this far with anyone else. She did trust him. She climbed onto the couch and knelt, facing the back, her legs spread, exposed. Nick teased the tip of the whip across her shoulders and down her back, tracing the line of her spine. He nudged the strips across her cheeks and along the edge of her buttocks. He eased the end along the length of her thigh until he dragged the tips along the sensitive backs of her knees. Nick kneeled and traced the same path with his tongue. When he lapped the sensitive skin behind her knee, a thousand sensations, all of them good, danced along her nerve endings. She moaned and leaned forward, exposing herself fully.

With a featherlight touch, he twirled the leather strips against her nether lips and then drew the hard line of the crop up between her buttocks.

"Do you want me to stop?"

"No."

"Then tell me what you want because we're partners."

"Do it again."

This time he twirled higher, the cluster of thin strips tormenting her clit. He drew the rigid length of the quirt along her wet folds. His tongue followed the trail blazed by the riding crop. He lapped between her thighs and flicked his tongue against her clit.

"I thought it was so hot when you touched yourself with this the other night. But it's even hotter now. Does it make you hot, Serena?"

"Yes. Hot and wet."

"Trust me, baby, I know just how wet it makes you. And just how good you taste."

He nudged at her entrance with the thicker, blunt handle of the riding crop and she was eager for the smooth, rounded tip. He eased it in and back out, going a little further each time. She gripped the edge of the sofa.

"Enough." She reached behind her, wrapped her fingers around his rigid rod and guided him to her. She teased against him. "Now I want the real McCoy."

"Your pleasure—" he thrust inside her and she gasped, loving the way he filled her, the heat, the pulsing of his rod in her wet, slick chamber "—is my pleasure."

AFTERWARDS NICK lay on her bed, where they'd eventually wound up, his arm around her waist, her back against his chest, spooning.

Serena rolled to her back and searched his face. "Why'd you do it, Nick?"

"Why'd I do what?"

"Why'd you take the money?"

People—his parents, his brother, his former employer, his friends—had asked *how had he done it, what had he been thinking, didn't he know he might get caught, hadn't he been raised better,* but he hadn't realized that until now, oddly enough, no one had ever asked him *why.*

"It would sound so much better if I could tell you that my grandmother was about to be tossed on the street or that I had a crippled cousin who needed the money for a life-saving operation."

She sat up, pulling the sheet up with her, leaving only her lovely shoulders bare. She wrapped her arms around her knees. "Those all sound pretty good, but it was nothing like that, was it?"

He propped himself up on his elbow. He could lie to her. He wished he could lie to her. But they both deserved better. "No. You want it square?"

Her eyes took on that hard look she'd had when she'd taken her gun and ordered him against the wall. She was the cop, not the woman he'd just made love to. "I'm a big girl. I want it square. Why'd you take the money?"

"Because I could." The plain, unadorned truth.

She nodded and looked away from him. "That's what I thought."

"Hey Riggs, what's it like having a love slave?" Pantoni said the minute she walked into the room.

It was typical and she totally expected it, but

now she had to wonder if he had ulterior motives. She'd give them plenty of trash talk.

"He cleaned my apartment from top to bottom—even scrubbed out my toilet with a toothbrush," she said.

Harding looked as if he'd just caught a whiff of rotten fish. "Did he wear that dog collar you bought yesterday?"

"Yeah. That's the only thing I allow him to wear while he's at my place."

"No shit?" Bennigan laughed.

"This dude needs help," Harding said.

Pantoni laughed at Harding's disgust. "Don't sweat it, man, they'll like his dog collar when he gets to the big house."

Serena perched on the edge of Bennigan's desk that sat in the center of the room. "Nah. His collar has to stay with me. He can only wear it where and when I tell him to."

"And what does he get in return?" Bennigan asked, eyeing her legs.

Pantoni jumped in. "Don't you know anything, you schmoe? The dude gets off on her just bossing him around."

"How do you know so much about it, Pantyboy?" Harding asked.

"I did a little surfing to check it out—in case Riggs needed any help or advice."

"Right, you freakin' perve. So, let's hear your advice then," Harding said. Harding wasn't usually so testy and challenging.

"Riggs, if he shows up with a drug store bag asking you to play Nurse Betty, you better run like hell in the other direction." Pantoni smirked at all of them.

It sent Harding over the top. "What a maggot."

Serena spoke up. "He's a maggot 'cause he launders money. Just 'cause he's into a little S&M doesn't make him a maggot. It's a little out there, but it's not hurting anyone…well, except for him."

"Hey. I asked a question and I still haven't gotten an answer. What'd he get for wearing that dog collar and cleaning your house?" Bennigan said. And just why did he want to know so badly? Was he looking for a specific answer? Did he suspect she was making this all up?

She stood up and assumed the wide-legged stance she'd assigned to that roll. She looked down her nose at Bennigan, as if he was a wad of gum she'd found stuck on her shoe. "I spanked his ass until it was cherry-red."

"That's cold."

"That's sick."

Serena shrugged. "Hey, he likes it."

"What about you, Riggs? You must like it. You're looking happier than I've seen you in weeks." Pantoni cocked his head to one side. "I think she's got a glow about her, boys. You gonna start moonlighting down at the Diva Dungeon?"

"I'm about to crack this case. O'Malley's going down. And in the meantime, I've got a guy who's built like a Greek god cleaning my house in the buff. What's not to glow about?"

"O'Malley? I thought this guy was Malone," Harding said.

"Malone's an alias. I ran a check on O'Malley. He got caught embezzling but walked away when his employer didn't press charges. He didn't exactly get away with it, but he didn't do any time. Guess he thought he was slick and would work the money-laundering angle this time."

"Damn, you're good, Riggs," Bennigan said.

"I am, aren't I?"

"It all sounds good, but how you going to catch him?"

"I ordered him to come straight to my house from work today, so he should be bringing along his laptop and his day planner. The day planner info is what Debi Majette gave us. I'll send him down to the store on some errand and then I'll spend a few minutes with his stuff. Sooner or later, he'll slip up and when he does, I'll catch him. You know, basically criminals are stupid—"

"That's why the jails are so full," Bennigan and Pantoni finished in unison.

"You boys are learning."

As usual, Steve Shea sat in the background and didn't say much, but he laughed along with the rest of them. He seemed like a nice, quiet guy. She always felt guilty that his laugh got on her nerves.

* * *

"How do you live without a computer?" Nick asked her, setting his laptop up on the coffee table.

"Amazingly enough, I've managed to survive. Shocking, I know. Why would I spend money on something I don't really need when I could put that money into my house fund?"

He strung a phone line over to the outlet, then glanced over at her. "You really want your own place, don't you?"

"You have no idea how much. How many times did you move when you were a kid?"

"Never. Ma and Da still live in the house I grew up in. And they don't plan to move."

"Where's that?"

"Quincy. The neighborhood's not as nice as it used to be, but it's a good place."

"I know Quincy. It is a good place." Nick had grown up in a whole different world where people strung Christmas lights across the roofline of their house and had plastic Santas in the front yard. Where kids played stickball at the end of the street and neighbors looked out for one another.

"You moved a lot?"

"Pretty much every couple of months." She kept her voice light and noncommittal, careful not to let any of the loneliness of her childhood seep through. They'd never stayed in one place long enough for her to make friends. She'd spent seventeen years in Cleveland and knew one person there to call—her mother. And she really didn't want to discuss it. "Is that phone connection working for you?"

"DSL or broadband would be better, but if dial-up's all you've got, well, it'll be slow, but it'll work." Though Nick hadn't pursued the previous conversation she knew he didn't miss much.

"Okay, do your stuff, O'Malley."

Serena watched him work. His brow was knit in concentration, but his eyes were alight. He obviously loved this.

"Hey, take a look at this."

Serena leaned over his shoulder, willing herself to ignore the scent of his aftershave and the heat of his skin next to hers. Nick scrolled through several screens and Serena began to see a pattern emerge, but only after he'd pointed it out. Very subtle, very difficult to detect. "So, it looks as if Transitor and Amberton are dummy companies."

"It certainly looks that way to me," he said.

Serena perched on the sofa arm. "That's a major portion of the puzzle in place. Now if we could just get a fix on Nick Malone."

"Phone book? Bank records? Internet search?"

"Tried all of that. No luck. This guy's like a shadow."

"Birth records?" he said.

"Birth records?"

"Yeah. Even criminals aren't hatched, Serena. You know approximately how old he is so go in and do a search on birth records."

"Damn. I should have thought of that. You're a genius."

"Why don't we wait until we see if it nets us anything? Then you can consider me a genius." He grinned at her and she felt the strong tug of attraction, the tantalizing heat that was never far away when Nick was around.

Within a few seconds, he'd accessed the public records of Massachusetts. "Of course there's always the possibility he was born in another state, but it's worth a try."

Bingo. One Nicholas Joseph Malone born on August 12, 1975, to Angelina Boscow Malone and Thomas Raymond Malone. They copied down the information. Nick switched to another screen and searched a residential cross-reference for both of the listed parents. A. Boscow Malone lived across the city in a modest home. No Thomas Raymond Malone or any configuration of the initials showed up.

Nick aimed a high-five her way. "Even criminals have mothers. And if this guy's got 'MOM' tattooed on his butt, he's a mama's boy. He'll show up sooner or later."

"Go back and search the corporate registrations for any listings under Boscow," she said, following a hunch.

A couple of key strokes and the cursor was blinking. The same two corporations Nick had found earlier all had a Joseph M. Boscow as a corporate officer.

Serena felt like doing a happy dance—except she was a terrible dancer. She contented herself with a satisfied smile. "Fancy that. Slick Nick's middle name, Joseph, and his mother's maiden name, Boscow. Ten to one says he's Slick Nick's uncle and the brains behind the whole operation."

"Forget it. I've lost enough bets lately and I'm sure you're right. Damn, we're a good team."

"It's too bad you've got a criminal history— you'd make one heck of a cop. You're really good at this."

He caught her wrist. "Come here and I'll show you what else I'm really good at."

Good grief. He only had to touch her and heat bloomed low in her belly and spiraled through her. She wanted him. She was ready to touch and be touched, to ride one of those orgasmic highs Nick was so good at producing. But she should really wrap up work first. She gathered her waning willpower into a protest. "But we need a plan."

O'Malley tugged her onto his lap and the thick ridge of his erection played against her buttocks. "Baby, I've got your plan right here."

Her panties were warm and wet within seconds. There were plans—she pressed against him and anticipation hummed through her—and then there were plans.

11

TWO NIGHTS LATER, SERENA handed Nick the final dish to put on the table. He'd essentially moved in after that first night. It had seemed like the safest option. She knew she could protect him better if she had him with her. Oddly enough, even though he didn't have any training, she'd gotten the impression he thought he was watching out for her by being there. Sweet, but misguided.

They'd developed a rhythm of working together. It was a little eerie how well they connected and tuned into one another.

Serena turned off the stove and joined him at the table. Nick never sat before she did. He always stood, waiting for her. It was a little weird, but there was also a courtliness to it, a gallantry, that secretly thrilled her.

They ate in silence for a few minutes before Nick broached the subject Serena knew had been brewing since their discussion the previous evening.

"Can we do this? Can we shut down Boscow and Malone and nail the mole in the department by ourselves?" Nick asked.

Serena knew he was worried. He'd been far too quiet and subdued tonight. "We don't have any choice. We have to," she said.

She tried to instill a confidence in her voice she knew he needed to hear. She wished she could take what she had to Harlan Worth, but she just couldn't risk it. There was too much at stake.

With a start, she realized that the crushing sense of aloneness that had swamped her when she'd first suspected a department mole no longer plagued her. In the short while since she'd met him, Nick had become not only a lover, but an ally and a confidant as well. If she were less pragmatic and more of a romantic, she might begin to fancy herself in love with O'Malley. Luckily, Serena was neither. Not to mention O'Malley was a criminal.

She'd anticipated having to cover him and do her job, but he had more than pulled his own weight. Serena wasn't sure how far along on the case she'd be right now, if not for him. "We just have to plan carefully and cover all the angles. We can do it."

Tonight there wasn't a teasing glint lighting his eyes. He wore a cloak of somberness. "I should go in on my own. Alone. You can back me up."

"What? That's crazy." Honestly, the thought of putting O'Malley on the line made her crazy…well, more accurately, nauseous. He might think like a criminal, but he had no idea just how vicious a cornered rat could be.

"You could get hurt," he said. He looked positively miserable. "I don't want you going in there without any kind of backup."

He was worried about *her?* The very thought sent a queer jolt through her nervous system. How naive could he possibly be? "That's crazy. I'm the one with the training. I want you to stop and think long and hard about something. These guys are setting you up. If their plan works, it wouldn't be a situation like you had before, where you got your wrist slapped, a big dose of public humiliation and you walked away scot free. No. They plan for you to take the fall and it'll be a big fall. This could net you thirty to forty years in prison. With your prior, you might get out in twenty with good behavior."

There was a stubborn cast to his mouth she'd never seen before.

She stabbed her fork at him. "Do you hear what I'm saying, Nick? You would be fifty, maybe even sixty years old. That portion of your life gone." She nearly wept at the thought. "Your parents could be dead by then. You'd be pretty old to get married and start a family. Without blinking, they've planned to take away your life. They don't play nice. They don't play fair." She put her fork down. She wasn't hungry any more.

"I understand what we're up against." He laughed, but it was with harshness, not his usual good humor. "I guess I'm smarter than I look." He crooked a finger beneath her chin and tilted her face up to his. "Careful there, Serena, or I might think you care." His tone held a hint of mockery, but there was also a hint of a question and vulnerability in his eyes.

Her heart slammed against her ribs and her breath seemed to desert her. "Of course I care. If something happens to you, I'm in this by myself."

The wry twist of his lips that passed for a smile mocked both of them. "And here I was thinking you were just another hard-nosed, cold-hearted cop who didn't care."

"Very funny. Slick Nick is going to be our best shot. I'm sure he's the weakest link. We approach him, isolate him and promise him immunity in exchange for the cop and his uncle."

"And what if he won't cooperate?"

"We'll stake out his mother's place. If a guy even remotely resembling you shows up, we get a make on his car and I tail him. Sooner or later, he'll have to go home. Then it's just a matter of breaking him down."

He pushed his chair away from the table and glared at her. "You're planning to use the boots and the whip, aren't you?"

What was his problem? "Of course. He'll be putty in my hands."

"That's what I'm afraid of. Let me go in to talk to him."

"Absolutely not. The key to him caving is to exploit his weakness. Me in thigh-high leather boots with a whip telling him to put on a dog collar, that's his weakness. Not some guy threatening to beat him up."

He stood up and paced from the table to the kitchen doorway and back. "I just don't like to think about you alone with him in that outfit."

Oh. He was seriously hot when he was pissed. Of course, he pretty much had that seriously hot thing down all the time.

"Careful, Nick, I might think you care." She tossed his own words back at him, wavering between being flattered and being annoyed by his attitude.

"Well, if something happens to you, who would I go to? Who would I trust? I'd be in this alone."

She stood and closed the gap separating them. She slid her hands down his chest and felt his heartbeat galloping beneath her fingertips. "You know what I think? I think you're jealous that Slick Nick is going to see the boots and outfit."

Within seconds, he had her pinned against the dining room wall, his hands shackling her wrists at her side. Adrenaline and heat flashed through her. His breath, hot and ragged, whispered across her skin. "You're damn right I'm jealous. I can't stand to think about him touching you like this." He plied his thumb along the fullness of her lower lip and she trembled inside. "Or this." He skimmed his knuckles over her neck and across her breastbone, his touch light but electrifying. "Or kissing you like this." He feathered his lips down her neck and across her shoulder with the most delicate of kisses, gossamer touches that shattered her. It took a moment for her to gather her wits enough to speak.

"I assure you, he won't even lay one finger on me." He covered her breast with his mouth, his teeth teased against her distended nipple through her shirt and bra. Desire weighted her limbs, filling her with a sweet, hot lethargy. "But just to make sure we've got the bases covered, why don't you show me all the things you don't want him to do to me?"

SERENA WAITED in the hotel lobby. Men were so stupid. So predictable. Well, she shouldn't generalize. O'Malley wasn't stupid. She thought about his willingness to take off his pants for her and smiled. He was predictable.

Sure enough, Nick Malone had shown up at his mother's house for Sunday dinner. Whether it was the appeal of a good pot roast or familial devotion, she wasn't sure, but a man who bore a nodding resemblance to O'Malley but tended to dress like a gigolo had shown up at the residence of one Angelina Boscow Malone. Serena would bet her life—and she pretty much was—that it was Slick Nick.

She and O'Malley had tailed Malone from his mother's to a north side apartment, then to a bar, where she'd "bumped" into him. Now, half an hour later, she stood waiting in a hotel lobby for a room. O'Malley had helped wire her and also outfitted her with a homing device in her purse. For a rookie, he'd done a good job of tailing them. Now, he was stationed between her and Malone—his dark hair lightened to a gray, thick glasses obscuring his eyes, a perpetual slump rounding his shoulders—reading a copy of the *Wall Street Journal*. He looked like an aging accountant no one would like at twice, waiting for someone in the lobby.

She had to hand it to Malone, the hotel was nice, not a dive as she'd expected. He'd been careful not to take her back to his apartment and he'd hailed a cab instead of taking his car. Just as she'd suspected, Slick Nick had been desperate for a little dom action. She'd only had to leave the tasseled end of her whip peeking out of her handbag and he'd taken the bait—hook, line and sinker.

He'd introduced himself as Nick Davenport, and she'd told him her name was Angelina Wright. She'd taken a chance that since his mother's name was Angelina and he had a "MOM" tattoo on his ass that he liked to have spanked, that the name angle would be yet one more lure. Apparently it was. She'd seen the flicker in his eye and didn't even want to consider the oedipal inferences. Malone should invest in a good therapist. He had some serious issues.

Slick Nick struck her as such a pathetic loser that she almost felt sorry for him. But then she reminded herself he'd gladly snatch the best years of O'Malley's life without hesitation and her sympathy flew out the window. She couldn't wait to nail him.

He walked toward her, room key in hand, then grasped her elbow and herded her toward the elevator. "Our room is this way, Mrs. Smith."

She waited until the elevator closed behind them and then turned a glacial stare on him. "I didn't give you permission to touch me."

He dropped her arm and scuttled to the other side of the elevator like a cockroach. "I'm so sorry. It won't happen again, Angelina."

She looked at him as if he was scum. "See that it doesn't."

She maintained a haughty attitude and he remained suitably cowed for the remainder of the elevator ride and the short trip down the hall to the room. O'Malley wouldn't be far behind and then he'd station himself outside the room.

The hotel door closed behind them and she immediately took charge. Let him see up front that she was boss. She'd worn a dress that zipped up the front. She unzipped it now to reveal the short leather skirt and leather bustier. O'Malley would be turning inside out knowing she was in here with this dirtbag. Malone was practically foaming at the mouth.

She'd noted the outline of a gun beneath the cut of his suit jacket. She'd bet anything he was packing heat in an ankle strap, too.

"I think you've been a very naughty boy, Nicky. Angelina thinks you need to be punished."

She pulled her whip out of her purse and

stalked toward him. "Get on your knees when I'm talking to you."

He dropped like a load of bricks. He looked up at her, his eyes bright with sexual heat. "Don't look at me. I haven't told you to look at me." He immediately trained his eyes on the carpet.

"Very nice. Very good. Look at me now." She pulled out the dog collar and his eyes lit up like a kid at Christmas with a new toy. "I'm feeling generous today, so I'm going to let you wear this." She dangled the studded collar from the end of her finger. "But it better be the only thing you're wearing when you come out of the bathroom." She tossed the dog collar onto the floor at her feet. "Now crawl over here to get it."

Malone crawled. She stepped on the collar just as he reached for it. "Anything other than the collar and the party's over. Got it?"

He answered without looking at her. "Got it."

She moved her foot. "Good. Now hurry before I get bored and leave."

He hurried into the bathroom on all fours. In less than three minutes he was back, naked except for the dog collar. And yeah, Debi Majette didn't have a perception problem. That was one itty-bitty penis. Anyone who'd ever seen the two men naked would never mistake O'Malley for Malone. Poor guy. No wonder Malone had problems. In a world of frankfurters, bratwurst and salamis, he sported a cocktail wienie.

She almost felt guilty for where she was about

to go, but then she thought about the dirty money Malone didn't hesitate to launder and O'Malley languishing in a prison cell and she no longer hesitated to do what was necessary.

"Get over here and if you're good I'll give you the punishment you deserve." None of that made sense to her, but she'd pulled it right out of a dominatrix role-play book. And she must've said just the right thing because Malone crawled across the floor like an eager puppy. She slapped the whip against her boot and he quivered. Sheesh. She stalked around him, continuing to slap her whip against her boot. There it was, right cheek, a heart with "MOM" in the middle.

This was definitely the man of the hour. She'd found Slick Nick Malone.

Now, she just needed a little cooperation.

"Bad boys need to be tied up, don't you think?" She trailed the edges of the whip over his bare buttocks. "You'd like that, wouldn't you?" She brought the whip down with a sharp snap, the sound resounding against his bare flesh.

"Yes." It was more in response to what she'd done than an answer to her question.

"Would you like more of that?"

"Yes. More."

"Then lie flat on the floor and put your hands out in front of you."

Within seconds she had his hands shackled together, the cuffs wrapped around a rung at the base of the table. Malone wasn't going anywhere until she got the information she wanted.

She planted her booted stiletto heel in the small of his back. "I've waited a long time to meet you, Slick Nick."

He looked over his shoulder at her with surprise and not a little bit of panic. She ground the point of her heel into him. "I didn't tell you to look at me." He quickly averted his eyes. "Now, I'm feeling expansive…that means generous, so I'm going to allow you to speak."

"Who are you?"

"That's all a matter of perception and cooperation, Nicky. I can be your worst nightmare, or I can be a fantasy come true." She thwacked him with the quirt. "Or maybe I'm a little bit of both, huh?"

She felt like life imitating art in a B film noir. She lifted her boot from his back and stood, legs akimbo, straddling him. She leaned forward and affected a soothing tone. "See, Nicky, you have something I want and…" she slid the striated leather along his spine and didn't miss the shiver that followed in its wake "…I'm sure I have something you want. But if you don't give me what I want, then I can't give you what I think you deserve. You've got to earn it."

"How do I do that?"

She continued as if he hadn't spoken.

"I bet I know one of your fantasies, Nicky. See I know all about you. I know what goes on in your head. I know what you want. I know what you like. I bet you've got this fantasy of a big bad she-bitch cop who takes you in for questioning and gets a little rough with you. She handcuffs you to a table and when you give her what she wants, she rewards you with a cat-o'-nine. That gets your engine running, doesn't it, Nicky?"

Actually, it was a rhetorical question because from where she stood, she could see it revved his little engine. It was a lucky guess, but that had been a favorite fantasy she'd run across several times in her research.

"Yes. Yes, that does."

"Now, the flip side is your worst nightmare. You're terrified of waking up one morning and finding out your uncle Joseph or your cop friend are no longer protecting you. Isn't that your worst nightmare—being abandoned by Joseph or better yet betrayed by the cop you've bought?"

"Joseph would never do that."

She noted he hadn't denied the cop. "Maybe he wouldn't, but you really can't know for sure, can you? But I wouldn't be too sure of your friend the policeman. You know you can't trust him. He'll take your money, but he really despises you. How do you think I found you?"

Serena wasn't sure what happened, but one second she was standing over him and the next second Malone bucked and swept his powerful legs beneath her. She went down with a hard thunk, landing flat on her back, all the air knocked out of her. His legs pinned her beneath him.

"What do you think about that you she-bitch cop? Who's in charge now?" Malone barked.

Serena could only lie on the floor and gasp, unable to catch her breath.

SHIT. Something had gone wrong. Bad wrong. Adrenaline surged through O'Malley's body, galvanizing him like an electric current. A crash followed by Malone's sneering comment. Malone was dead if he'd hurt Serena. A lethal calm came over him and within seconds he'd picked the lock the way Serena had taught him and was in the room, coming in low and feinting right toward the bathroom.

Malone was handcuffed to the table base. Serena lay pinned beneath him. Why in the hell hadn't he insisted on a real gun instead of the stun gun she'd armed him with? But Malone wouldn't know that.

"Get off her before I blow your balls up into your belly, shit bag," Nick said, training his stun gun on Malone who turned to look at him.

Suddenly Serena brought her knee up and drove her stiletto heel back and down. Malone howled in pain and Serena rolled to her side and stood. "One nut just went north. How about shutting the door behind you, O'Malley? And thanks, that was timely. He shifted his weight when you sailed in. Nice job."

Nick closed the door. Malone lay sobbing on the ground in agony. That must've hurt like hell.

She motioned him to stand to the side. His woman was magnificent.

"Now where were we? Oh, yeah, we were talking about our mutual friend at the department, which seems to be a very touchy subject for you."

Snot and tears ran down Malone's face and he wiped his nose against the carpet. Christ, that was disgusting. Nick would never walk barefoot in a hotel room again.

"That bastard. I told Jo-Jo we couldn't trust him. I hate that bastard."

Serena sat on the edge of the bed and looked down at Malone, her lethal heel only inches from his face. She had the intimidation factor down to an art. "That's okay. He hates you as well. He just likes your money. And with you and Jo-Jo looking at several years of bonding in the federal pen, well, your money's not looking so good to him now."

"I'd kill him if I could. And Jo-Jo's going to blame me for this. He always blames me."

"Nicky, you have so much power right now. Think about it. You know what's worse than killing a cop? Sending a cop to prison. They're really not very popular with the other inmates."

"Jo-Jo'll kill me…or my mother. That's the way he works."

"Possibly. Actually it sounds very probable unless you buy yourself some immunity by cooperating."

"He killed my father when I was fourteen. I

overheard him talking about it afterwards. He never knew that I knew."

Nick saw a flash of pity cross Serena's face but she continued to press Malone. "Of course he knew. He wanted you to know and he wanted you to keep that terrible secret and let it eat at you and intimidate you. It meant that he owned you. But he doesn't have to own you anymore, Nick. Give us Jo-Jo, give us the cop and we'll give you a new life." Serena softened her voice and Nick knew she was talking to Malone person to person. "And there's no statute of limitations on murder. Work with me and I promise he'll stand trial and answer for killing your father."

"I can't give you a positive ID on the cop because I've never seen him or met him. I've only ever talked to him over the phone."

"Phone's good. Phone works. Which phone?"

"He calls me on my cell."

"So, you'd recognize his voice?"

"In a heartbeat. I especially hate that laugh of his, like fingers scraping down a chalkboard."

She looked both sad and relieved and Nick knew that Malone had just identified the traitor for her. She looked at Nick and yanked her head toward the bathroom. "Would you bring Nick his clothes and give me his weapons, please? He needs to get dressed so we can take a ride."

HARLAN PULLED her into his office, his blue eyes sober. "You did good work, Riggs. Damn good work considering you were on your own."

She knew what he meant, but she had to set him straight. "I wasn't on my own. I partnered with O'Malley."

"Well, the two of you did damn fine work."

"Thanks." She and O'Malley had made a helluva team. Dammit. She still couldn't believe Malone had caught her off guard that way and pinned her. Odds were she would've got herself out of the situation sooner or later, but O'Malley's entry had definitely meant sooner.

"You look done in."

"I'm tired." She had woken Harlan up and after he'd listened to her story he'd met her and O'Malley in an unused evidence room in the basement where they'd spent the night poring over phone records. They now had a solid case. The last remaining step was a positive voice ID and they'd laid the groundwork for that by wiretapping Malone's cell phone. Malone was sitting in a very small room, guarded by a very big officer. Malone had been just another day at work, but this…this takedown of another cop…the thought made her nauseous.

"You know you don't have to stay for this. I can make the arrest without you."

"I'm not that tired."

"Listen, Riggs, I know this isn't easy for you…"

"It's my bust, Harlan. I won't screw it up."

"It is your bust and I never thought you would."

Serena turned to get the party started and Harlan stopped her at the door. "Riggs."

"Yeah?"

"You're a helluva cop."

"Thanks." She walked out of Harlan's office. The boys were all at their desks. She pushed aside the thought that things would never be the same. She wasn't the one that had set this ball in motion.

"What's up, Cruella De Vil? Spanked any booty lately?" Pantoni mouthed off.

Yeah. Pantoni better have some damn good answers to give her. Later.

She dropped into her chair and didn't have to feign exhaustion. "This case sucks. I'm back to another big fat zero."

Bennigan chewed on the end of an unlit cigar. "What about O'Malley? Isn't he your guy? I thought you were going to be taking him down soon."

"O'Malley's too stupid to pull anything off. He can't be my guy."

"So, you've been spanking his ass for a week and he's not even your perp? You go, baby!" Pantoni positively chortled.

Steve Shea sat quietly eating a donut and drinking a cup of coffee. Serena eyed the coffee with longing. "If you guys weren't buttwipes, one of you would get me a cup of coffee instead of giving me a hard time."

"Hey, babe, you're confused. I ain't your freaking love slave," Pantoni said.

"Yeah, maybe you should bring that pathetic boy toy to work with you," Harding said, shaking his head in disgust.

Shea stood. "I'll be right back. You take it black, right?"

"Yeah, thanks, Steve."

Bennigan walked out of the room without comment.

"So, whatcha gonna do now?" Pantoni asked.

Serena shrugged and appeared nonchalant but inside her gut churned. "I guess I'll see what goes down in the next day or so. How's your fraud case going?"

She pretended to listen, all the time waiting for the signal. Harlan walked out of his office and gave her an imperceptible nod. It was done.

Bennigan walked back in the room, zipping his pants. For Christ's sake, couldn't he take care of that in the bathroom? Shea followed with her coffee and put it on her desk.

"Thanks, Steve."

"No problem."

Harlan moved closer into the room. Serena stood and slipped a cuff onto one of Shea's wrists. Harlan quietly took his other arm and she cuffed it as well. "Steve Shea, you are under arrest. You have the right to remain silent…" She had to hand it to Shea, he didn't resist and while she finished reciting the Miranda all the commotion came from the other guys.

"What the hell?"

"Jesus, what are you doing?"

"If this is a joke, it's not funny."

Harlan and Serena ignored the other guys. Harlan relieved Shea of his weapon and plucked his cell phone from his top pocket. "He called Malone while he was getting your coffee."

She'd been so right, arrogance had been his downfall, but she didn't feel vindicated, she felt sick with betrayal. "Why, Steve? How could you do this to all of us?"

"I don't know what you're talking about," he said, his eyes flat and cold. For all the times she'd brought in the bad guys, this was different. Steve had traded in his white hat. At that moment, something inside her that believed in innate goodness died.

Harlan shook his head. "I'll send O'Malley up," he said and led Shea away. Serena nodded and sank into her chair, as winded as she had been last night when Malone had knocked her on the floor.

Pantoni, Bennigan and Harding crowded around her, demanding answers. Considering a man's life had just unraveled through his own misjudgment and the fabric of the department had been destroyed, it took a relatively short time to lay it out.

The guys were stunned and Serena was exhausted and tired of deceit and lies so she asked Pantoni the question that had nearly given her a freaking ulcer. "You were wasted at McCaffrey's last week and told me you'd betrayed me and that you'd never meant to hurt me. What was that all about?"

"You won't like it."

"Everything's relative. Now that I know you aren't the one selling out the department, it can't be too bad."

Bennigan and Harding stared Pantoni down. "What've you done to Serena?"

"I was talking to Francesca a couple of weeks ago about how we could maybe work things out. She told me it was too late. She'd been seeing someone. You guys know how I can get. You know that male pride thing. Anyway, I went a little crazy and told her I'd been sleeping with Serena."

Serena wasn't sure whether to laugh or cry or punch him. So instead she said, "You wish," only because she knew he'd never had any designs on her.

"Guess she told you."

"You hoser. Serena's lucky Francesca didn't come up here and kick her ass," Bennigan said.

"Yeah, well, I guess she doesn't care that much," Pantoni said. "You aren't even mad?"

"I'm too tired to be mad, Joe. And too relieved that it was Shea and not you. Not any of you." For one emotionally overfraught dangerous moment she almost told them what they meant to her. Luckily she caught herself in time. They knew and there was no need to scare the hell out of them. They'd think she was having a psychotic episode or something if she got all mushy. "But you better set that straight with 'Cesca or *I'm* going to kick *your* butt."

"You gonna wear those boots to do it?"

"I'm not playing with you Panty-oni. Take care of it."

"All right, all right, I'll take care of it."

O'Malley appeared in the doorway. "You ready?"

She stood and the boys moved with her, silently taking measure of O'Malley, squaring their shoulders and putting on their bad-ass cop faces.

Nick stepped forward and held out his hand. "I'm Nick O'Malley. It's a pleasure to meet you."

The guys all shook his hand. Bennigan slapped him on the shoulder. "Thanks for backing up Riggs."

"It was my pleasure." And then because Nick seemed to be a very smart man who realized he was about to face a ton of well-intentioned interrogation, he slung his arm around Serena's shoulders and herded her toward the door. "Let's go home."

NICK COULDN'T STAND it any longer. She'd been in there forever. How long could she possibly shower? He knocked on the door.

"Come in." The running water muffled her voice. He didn't wait for a second invitation. He shouldn't have waited at all, but been in there from the start.

Sure, he had confidence in her, but he'd never been so scared in his life as he'd been when she'd disappeared into that hotel room with Malone. Nothing, not prison, not losing the next twenty to thirty years of his life, would have been as bad as losing her. Without her, none of that mattered anyway.

He pulled aside the curtain. She stood beneath the ongoing spray, statue-still. "You okay?" he asked.

"Yeah. Sometimes, afterwards, I feel as if I can't quite get clean." Her hair hung in wet rat tails about her face, a smudge of mascara shadowed beneath one eye. With the freckles across her nose, the sluice of water across her naked breasts and her belly, the drenched curls between her thighs, she was breathtakingly beautiful. But an ineffable sadness clung to her, residing in the depths of her eyes.

"It's all the exposure to scum. You can't help but feel like some of it rubs off on you," he said.

"I think it does."

He stepped into the shower with her, heedless of his clothes. "Nick." Despite her protesting tone, she willingly stepped into his arms. He smoothed his hand over her head and pressed a kiss to her temple. "I'm sorry about Steve Shea."

"Thank you. I hate it that Steve did what he did, but I'm so grateful it wasn't Worth, Pantoni, Harding or Bennigan. That would've been…difficult."

Difficult was an understatement. Nick suspected it would have crushed her, perhaps damaged her beyond repair, had it been one of those four. They were like family to her. Because her own family hadn't been much good to her.

Nick couldn't imagine being in Serena's position. He'd always had the full support and love of two parents who approached life with dignity, respect and an indefatigable work ethic. He'd grown up in a lower middle-class neighborhood of small tidy homes and a sense of close-knit community.

She'd mentioned moving often. Nick had read between the lines. He felt sure she'd grown up in one low-income, rent-subsidized housing project after another. He couldn't imagine the transience of moving so often. He couldn't imagine the humiliation of having a father in jail. He had a new appreciation, a new depth of understanding, of the impact his actions had on his family.

"Did you know Steve Shea well?"

"He was quiet. Kept to himself. It's really torn the department apart. I hope none of the guys blame me."

"That's ridiculous. Shea put a price on each one of your heads. You did a good thing. Try not to think about it. Tomorrow's a new day, a fresh start."

For her. For them. He was bursting inside to tell her how he felt. He wanted to drop to one knee, here, now, and tell her she was his sun and his moon, she was what he'd been waiting a lifetime for without realizing it. He wanted to tell her he loved her.

But today had been stressful enough—she was stretched as tight as a Stradivarius. Tomorrow, a new day—their new beginning when they didn't have to see one another because of the Nick Malone case—was soon enough.

For now, he'd love her, comfort her, show her with his actions where his heart lay.

12

"GET IN BED. I'll bring you a glass of wine and some cheese and crackers," Nick said, turning back her comforter, wearing a pair of those tighty whities she hadn't thought were very sexy the first time she'd seen them in his drawer, but had decided were very hot indeed after seeing them on him.

She considered arguing because she really didn't need anyone to take control and take care of her, but then thought better of it. Maybe he wasn't as much taking control as he was just being nice and thoughtful. She climbed into bed, wearing her very unsexy but very comfortable T-shirt from her days in the police academy and pulled the sheet up. "Thanks. That sounds good. There are some rosemary crackers in the cabinet that go well with the Irish cheddar and there's a chardonnay pinot grigio blend already chilled."

"Should I slice the cheese into squares or rectangles?" O'Malley asked.

Serena laughed at him and herself. "Okay. I'm sorry. I'm beginning to recognize I do have some control issues. Please bring me whatever cheese, crackers and wine you choose."

"Coming right up." Nick paused in the doorway and glanced over his shoulder, looking sexier than any man had a right to. She felt a sweet tension snake through her. "You know sometimes giving someone else the control is a very good thing."

Her nipples tightened just thinking about the other night when she'd handed over her riding crop. Serena ached for Nick, wanted him with a depth and fierceness that superseded anything she'd ever felt before. She was greedy. One last time she wanted to make love to him. One last time she wanted him to take her to a place where everything was good.

Somewhere along the line she'd done the un-thinkable and fallen in love with Nick O'Malley. Maybe it had first started when she'd heard him professing his lust for her to a blow-up doll. Maybe it was when he'd blown five hundred bucks because he couldn't wait another day for her. Was it when he'd shown up with a bouquet of flowers and known he'd scared her to death? Was it the sex that took her somewhere out into the stratosphere? Was it when he looked at her and she could swear he knew her as well as she knew herself? Maybe it was when he'd come tearing into that room with a stun gun, hellbent on rescuing her. Or was it to-night when he'd stepped into the shower, fully clothed, because he'd sensed she needed him?

Dammit. He'd forced a partnership when she

didn't want a partnership. She was used to going it alone. And now she'd gotten used to the partnership. And what had her head been thinking to let her heart make such a stupid decision? Nick had some really wonderful qualities. He was smart, tender, loyal, and although it wasn't the most important aspect, she couldn't overlook that he was drop-dead gorgeous.

But over the past several days, plans—or, more specifically, the lack of them in her life—had smacked her in the face. And all the freaking talk about babies had smacked her in the face. She wanted the whole enchilada. She didn't just want a house, she wanted a home, complete with a reliable husband and a kidlet or two.

For all that she loved Nick, how could she do that? Marry a man and have children with him when she knew he had a criminal history? Not only did he have the history, he liked doing it, and he was damn good at it. All things not in his favor for the future. How would she explain it to their kids when Nick wound up in prison? How could she face them? She wouldn't join the legion of women who believed the love of a good woman could turn the tide in a man on the wrong path. Well, that was a mixed metaphor, but it didn't change what she knew. She'd lived that life, grown up that way. Not only did she deserve better, but her children deserved better than that situation.

Nick carried in a laden tray. He placed it on the

nightstand next to her. "I thought you might've gone to sleep."

"No. Just thinking."

"About?"

"Stuff." Not tonight. Tonight she wanted him one last time.

He handed her a glass of wine and took the other. "A toast…" he raised his glass, his blue eyes smiling, yet intense "…to partners."

She touched her glass to his. They had made a good team. "To partners." She sipped the wine.

"You've got to be exhausted."

"I'm better. The shower helped." Had it been the shower or had it been the comfort he'd extended? She didn't want to think about it now. She only wanted to feel the heat and press of his body on hers, in hers.

She placed her wine back on the table, then took his glass from him and put it beside hers. She linked her arms around his neck and pulled him down on top of her, intent on absorbing everything about him, his scent, the feel of his skin, the scrape of his five o'clock shadow, his weight. She wanted to melt inside with him one last time.

His mouth met hers, his lips cool and sweet from the wine. His kiss was tender, yet she sensed the same fierce want in him that she felt. He kissed his way down her throat and she melted inside. He paused to pull her T-shirt over her head. Once he'd tossed it to the floor, he took a sip of wine. He lowered his head and captured her nipple in his mouth. Serena gasped from the sensation of his wine-chilled mouth against her hot flesh.

Every movement brought her closer to the place she wanted to go. It wasn't just his mouth and tongue moving across her skin with such exquisiteness, the press of his pelvis against her, the weight of his erection against her thigh, the flexing of his muscles beneath her fingertips. It was the meeting of spirit and soul as well as flesh.

Nick plucked a condom off of the tray that held the cheese and crackers. He must've read her look. He smiled his smile that twisted her into knots as he removed his briefs and sheathed himself. "Hey, I was hoping you weren't asleep. I wanted to come prepared."

"I think you mean you were prepared to come."

"That too." He hovered between her thighs, his thick head nudging between her wet folds. "And what about you, my sweet Serena, are you prepared to come?"

"Yes." That one breathless word unlocked a wealth of sensation as he slid into her and his lips captured hers in an equally intimate kiss.

Then together they took each other to a place where spirit and flesh bonded, outside the realm of anything she'd ever known.

NICK OPENED his eyes, momentarily disoriented.

Serena regarded him from the open blinds in her bedroom, where the morning sun poured into the room. "Sorry to wake you so early, but I've got a busy day planned, lots of loose ends to tie up. If you want to go ahead and get dressed, I'll be in the kitchen putting on some coffee."

Nick tamped down the foreboding that rose inside him at her abrupt, dismissive tone. He'd only ever spent time with her in the evenings. Obviously she wasn't a morning person. He'd lie low until she'd had a caffeine infusion.

He didn't rush through getting dressed, leaving her ample time to brew her coffee and start a cup. She wandered back into the bedroom, a ceramic mug in one hand. "Oh, I thought you must've gone back to sleep."

"No. Just giving you a little space."

"Thanks. Can I offer you a cup before you leave?"

"That'd be great. I'm not in a big hurry. I'm pretty sure that after yesterday, I'm once again gainfully unemployed." He smiled.

She didn't smile back. "Yeah. I think that's pretty likely."

She moved past him without looking at him and made up her bed with military precision, not offering any other comments, steadfastly ignoring him. Nick embraced mornings, the fresh start of a new day, but his true love's early-morning social skills left something to be desired.

He covered the short distance from her bedroom to the kitchen and poured himself a cup of coffee. Amazing, how he'd learned where everything was and where everything belonged in a few short days. Actually, he felt as if he belonged.

She walked into the kitchen behind him. "I want you to know how much I appreciate your help with this case. I'm not so sure I would've had the same outcome without your help."

Nick winked at her and slid his arm around her waist, determined to coax her into a better humor. "I told you, we make a good team."

She slipped away from him and walked to the sink.

Keeping her back to him, she rinsed out her mug. "We worked well together." She turned around and wrapped her arms around her middle. "Good luck finding another job. You might want to do a background check on any job offers this time."

What the...? Nick put his coffee cup on the counter. He moved to stand before Serena, all but forcing her to look at him. "That sounded alarmingly close to a 'have a nice life' speech."

She shrugged and wouldn't meet his eyes. "Well, we wrapped up the case and you'll be busy and I'll be busy."

He cupped her chin in his hand, forcing her to meet his eyes. "I'm not that busy and I'm not talking about the case, but you know that, don't you?"

Her eyes matched her expression, cool and remote. "Let's not make this awkward for either one of us, Nick. We had really great sex together while we were thrown together by circumstances and now those circumstances have changed. End of story."

"End of story? You're not kidding?"

"Of course not. Why would I kid about this?"

"How about end of chapter? Beginning of next one? How about going out to dinner, going to a movie, catching a game at Fenway Park, strolling along Boston Harbor on a warm night in the moonlight? You know, those things that a real couple does instead of meeting up for sex?"

"That's not a good idea. It's best if we just leave well enough alone."

"Best for whom? I don't think it's best for you and I know it sure as hell isn't best for me. Last night, when you disappeared into that hotel with Malone, I've never known such fear. I could taste it, cold and heavy, against my tongue. I realized if something happened to you, the sun would never rise for me again, the moon would never lighten the dark night again, because you've become my moon and my sun and my stars. I love you, Serena. And at the risk of sounding like an egomaniac, I think you care about me, too."

"Nick, you're a nice guy, but this just wouldn't work."

"How would it not work? This hasn't been the best of circumstances and it's been working. Why wouldn't you give it a chance now?"

"I'm a cop. Even though you were never arrested, you committed a crime. You're a criminal. How does that work?"

The light went on for him. "This isn't about you being a cop. Not really, is it? It's about my past."

He ran a hand through his hair. "But that's exactly what it is—the past. I made a mistake. It's over. I won't be going there again."

"I don't believe it, Nick. Once a criminal always a criminal. I saw your face when you hacked into Malone's files. And do you know why you were so damn good at figuring it out? Because you think like a criminal."

"I know what I did was wrong. I would never do anything like that again."

"I've got some shocking news for you. I've heard that before. I've heard it growing up from my father and I hear it weekly at the station when wives, mothers, girlfriends come to bail them out. *I'm sorry, baby, it won't happen again. I'm a changed man.* And they genuinely are sorry and they are changed—until it happens again. Well, I'm sorry, Nick, but I don't believe it and I'm not willing to take that chance. I grew up hearing the same thing. I won't live that way as an adult. And here's the scary part, here's the reason I think you will do it again—you knew it was wrong the first time around. There was never any question about that. But you did it. And to quote you, you did it because you could."

"This isn't about me. This is about your father. It's all about your father. Every time you make an arrest, it's not about the guy you've just collared. You're punishing your dad, aren't you? You're letting him destroy you, bit by bit, piece by piece, day by day, because you're letting the bitterness eat at you and, sooner or later, it's going to destroy you. Don't let what's between you and him come between you and me. We have something special. I think we've found something few people are lucky enough to have." He poured the rest of the coffee down the drain. It tasted bitter now. "But this thing between you and your father, it's like a poisonous vine that's growing and strangling everything good—and that includes you."

SERENA GOT into her lonely bed and turned out the light. Damn Nick O'Malley. Even between her infrequent boyfriends, her bed had never seemed lonely. It was definitely lonely now. And she'd definitely get over it. She'd survived before O'Malley and she'd survive after him. Although, wasn't life about more than mere survival? Maybe, but that's what it ultimately came down to. She punched her pillow, angling for a more comfortable place to put her head. She needed a good night's sleep and she wasn't going to waste her time thinking about things she couldn't change…like Nick.

Serena looked through the bars at her father. Despite the years, he didn't look any older. She didn't want to be here. She didn't understand why she was here. She only knew she had to get out. She didn't belong in here. He did.

"Why am I here? You're supposed to be in here. Not me. I haven't done anything. Let me out of here, right now."

Her father had nothing to say. But then again, he'd never had anything to say that she could believe. But he stood outside her small, barred cell, looking up, shaking his head.

"What do you mean no? You've got to let me out." She grasped the bars. The iron remained cold and unyielding. "Please, I don't want to be in here." She reduced herself to pleading. "I don't like it. I never did anything to deserve this. Please, help me out. Give me the key. Just give me the key. You could at least do that for me."

He merely stood there, shaking his head, as cold and unyielding as the bars that contained her. Then, like a fog dispersing, her father disappeared.

She looked about her, but she was alone in her prison. What had she done that they'd locked her in solitary? She sank to the floor and wrapped her arms around her knees, desolate in her personal prison.

One by one, her mother, Harlan Worth, Pantoni, Bennigan, Trixie, even Jimmy, stood outside her cell. Her pleas for release, each time, fell on seemingly deaf ears, as they looked at her with sympathy but moved on without speaking.

Finally Nick O'Malley stood outside, looking at her, his brilliant blue eyes awash in sorrow and longing. She was almost too weary and despairing, but she lifted her head. "Help me, Nick. I don't belong in here. You told me you loved me once. Won't you please let me out?"

Nick shook his head, the same as her father, and the crushing disappointment nearly incapacitated her. But then, unlike those preceding him, he spoke. "The key is where it's always been." He looked up, the same as her father had, but he pointed to a spot above her head. "The key is where it's always been."

She looked up. A key, intricately detailed, hung suspended above her. She stood and reached. It dangled, just out of her reach. She looked at Nick, who waited on the other side. "I can't do it. I can't reach it. Help me, Nick. I love you. If I could just get out of here, we'd have a good life together."

She knew it with a certainty that made the elusive key all the more unattainable.

"You've got to jump for it. I'm right here, waiting for you, but if you want to get out, you have to take a leap."

NICK FINISHED the story and looked from Matt to AJ to Tim. For the first time in his memory, absolute silence reigned for a full minute at their table.

AJ spoke first. "Fact verification. Your boss tried to frame you, you've been working undercover with a cop who is not a sex therapist but who you were going at it with, and said cop dropped you like a used rubber 'cause you embezzled from Gleeson."

"That about sums it up."

"Forget Sabrina."

"Serena."

"Yeah. Whatever. Forget about her. Listen, my cousin's friend's sister just got back from Barbados. Hot, hot, hot. Blond, tanned and mongo tatas. I was supposed to meet her, but how about I have my cousin set you up with her instead?" Matt said.

Nick thought again that his friends might be buttheads, but when a guy was down, they really came through—in their way. Matt was willing to give up a date with mongo tatas for him. "Nah. I can't let you do that."

"It's cool, man. Really. You'll be over Selena by next week."

"It's Serena, you moron," Tim said.

"See, Nicky's got no business with her, 'cause I can't even remember her name."

"For God's sake, put a sock in it, Matt. You're sounding like me and it's making my head hurt. There's not room at the table for two of us to be as obnoxious as I am." AJ looked at Nick. "You're seriously messed up over this chick, aren't you?"

"She's the one."

"I'd say that's serious."

"I'd say that's messed up."

"I always thought Tim would be the first one to fall."

"He was, you moron. He's married."

"Oh, yeah."

"So you're out of the running because her old man's a jailbird and you committed a crime and she doesn't trust you not to do it again? It's a bitter irony—" *bitter irony from AJ?* "—that you, who has had women drop at your feet your whole life, is now rejected by the one woman you really want. That sucks, man."

Nick paused to savor the moment. It was a first. Finally, AJ said a situation sucked on his behalf instead of telling him he sucked. Just went to prove miracles happened every day. Of course, he could've definitely lived without the bitter irony being pointed out to him. "I'm not giving up. And I'm not waiting for anyone to fix this. I'm going to fix it myself. I'm going to prove to her I can stay clean."

"One problem, chief. How long is that gonna take? A month? A year? Five years?"

An idea began to gel in the back of his mind. "Give me a week." For the first time in days, he felt real hope rather than just empty optimism that bordered on denial. "You can't change a zebra's stripes, but you can teach it a new trick."

"That doesn't make any sense."

Nick laughed. "You'll see what I mean."

_13_

SERENA SAT ACROSS FROM Harlan Worth in his office. She didn't know any easy way to say what she needed to, so she put the folded paper on his desk, pushed it toward him and cut straight to the point.

"I'm leaving the force. That's my resignation."

Harlan paused in the unwrapping of his Twinkie. "You're a damn fine cop, Riggs. And you did a damn fine job on that last case. You busted your ass to make detective and now you're leaving?" He bit into the Twinkie and peered at her over the top of his reading glasses. Unfortunately, a little thing like a mouthful of cream filling never kept Harlan from talking. "You pregnant?"

"No. Why would you think that?" She looked down at her stomach. She might've put on a few pounds, but... "Do I look pregnant?"

"No. But you've been looking pretty damn miserable. So, I'm putting two and two together. You had the hunk hanging out at your house for a week, then you look miserable and you tell me you're leaving. I'm thinking you must be knocked up and got a bad case of morning sickness."

Serena laughed. "I'm not knocked up. But I've been giving it a lot of thought and I think I became a cop for the wrong reasons. I've been living in a vigilante state and that's not healthy."

Harlan nodded. "Being a cop is tough, even on a good day. If you're not careful, it can eat away at you, until there's nothing left. I've seen it happen. I'm not going to try and talk you out of it, but we're damn sure going to miss you."

"I'm going to miss you guys something fierce. Don't think you're actually going to be rid of me for good."

"What you going to do?"

"I'm going to culinary school."

"No kidding? To cook? Let me know if you need a taste-tester." He nodded toward the empty Twinkie wrapper. "Ya know I got gourmet taste."

Inside, Serena offered a sigh of relief. In his own way, Harlan had just offered his approval of her plan. And it was both exciting and scary to have actually said it aloud, to have given it validity.

"I'll be sure to keep that in mind."

"What you going to do for money, if you don't mind me asking? I'm sure you've got it figured out, but, ya know…I'm just asking."

"It's pretty obvious I don't spend a lot of money on being a glamour girl. I've got some money tucked away 'cause I've been saving for a down payment on a house. I figure if I'm about to be unemployed, I won't be buying a house anyway, and an education will be a good investment of my money. Plus, I thought I could do a little moonlighting for some of the detective agencies in town."

"You could always work part-time as a dominatrix at one of those clubs. They pull down good money."

"Nah. To each his own, but that's not my scene." Serena took a deep breath and then asked him the question that mattered the most. "Harlan, do you think that criminals can change? You and I both see the recidivism rate. It just doesn't seem likely."

"I'm old and I'm cynical and I'll have to tell you that it's possible, but not often probable. That said, I think people can do anything they set their mind to do. No one can change another human being to be what they want them to be. But everyone can change themselves if they want to. Does that make sense?"

"Yeah, it does."

"This wouldn't have anything to do with O'Malley, would it?"

Her heart hammered. Had O'Malley been involved? Had he been implicated and she simply didn't know it yet? "Yeah. Do you know something I don't?"

Harlan looked at her strangely. "No. I just thought I sensed a personal interest there."

She was punch-drunk in love and twice as frightened as she'd ever been in her entire life that she'd take a chance and he'd let her down. "There might be an interest."

Harlan eyed her over his glasses as if he knew she missed O'Malley so much she felt hollow inside. "Some people are saints, some people are sinners, but most people are a combination of the two. You've got to trust your gut. And sometimes expectations, our own and others', become a self-fulfilling prophecy."

NICK WAITED in the discreetly plush office of the building he used to work in. He'd stolen half a million dollars from Gleeson, once upon a time, so it was no surprise Gleeson left him cooling his heels. Actually, he'd been relieved Gleeson had agreed to see him at all.

Sylvia, the big man's executive secretary, kept looking at him as if he were Lazarus, risen from the dead. She answered her phone and then stood. "Mr. Gleeson will see you now."

Nick crossed the room. Sylvia ushered him through one of the paneled double doors and closed it behind him. Gleeson looked up from his desk but didn't rise and didn't offer to shake hands. Nick was cool with that. He doubted if he would've either had he been in the other man's place.

"O'Malley."

"Mr. Gleeson. Thank you for agreeing to see me today."

"Sit. It's not every day I get a call from a man

who embezzled from me. I have to admit I'm curious about what you could possibly want to discuss with me."

Nick sat in a tufted leather chair and cut to the chase. Gleeson was a busy man and he figured he had less than five minutes, if that, to state his case. "One of the things we never talked about was why I took the money. I think most people assumed it was greed. That played a part in it, but if you'll remember, I hadn't spent any of it when you caught me. The main reason I took your money, Mr. Gleeson, was because I could. I don't work for you anymore and I'd like to thank you once again for not pressing charges, but here's the thing, there are lots more people like me out there. A friend of mine pointed out that most criminals are repeat offenders. She also pointed out that I tend to think like a criminal. I need a job. I'm not really sure who would trust me for a good job at this point. So, I'm going to work with what I have going for me. If you're hunting a terrorist or you want to protect yourself from a terrorist, who's the best person to have on your side? Another terrorist. I want to tell companies where they're vulnerable."

Gleeson templed his fingers and speared Nick with a laser-sharp gaze. "You're telling me you want a company to pay you to hack into their files?"

"Yes. That's it in a nutshell. I expose and fix their weaknesses. And if they've already been hit, I help track it down for them."

"And how do they know you won't rip them off while you're in there?"

"Because then I'd be right where I am now, damn near unemployable—except in a worse spot, because then I'd be a repeat offender. Plus, I'd be biting the hand that feeds me."

Gleeson crossed his arms over his chest. "And what's this got to do with me?"

"An attempt at restitution." Nick reached into his briefcase and pulled out a document. He placed the bound information packet on the desk and slid it across to Gleeson. "That's a report on your company. I've identified several weak spots, despite your firewalls. I've also recommended corrective actions."

Gleeson glanced at the report but didn't pick it up. "How current is this?"

"It's current as of two days ago. Has anyone come to you flagging anything in your system?"

"No."

"If I can get in there undetected, trust me, there are others out there who will figure it out."

"I want my guys to take a look at this. Authenticate it."

"Absolutely. They can implement my suggestions, or, at your go-ahead, I can take care of it for you."

"And how much does this cost me?"

Nick shook his head. "This one's on me. It's the least I can do. However, if you'd give me a recommendation I'd appreciate it. If you don't, I'd certainly understand."

"What could possibly carry more weight than an endorsement from the man you ripped off? You've got balls and brains, O'Malley, two traits I admire in a man." He thumbed through the report. "If this is verified, I'll endorse you."

"I DIDN'T ORDER another beer," Nick said as Cherry put the brew in front of him. Why would he have ordered a single when he and his buddies had a pitcher on the table? And he hadn't even had a sip of the one in front of him. Drinking too much when he was depressed seemed like a bad habit to start.

"Compliments of the lady at the bar."

Nick, his back to the bar, turned and looked over his shoulder. There were women at the bar. None, however, seemed interested in him or their table. "Which lady?"

Cherry raised her hands, palms upward. "She was just there. Maybe she's in the ladies' room. I don't know. She just told me to bring you a beer, so I did."

"Fine. Just leave it." He turned back around. He wasn't going to argue with her and he didn't really care who'd sent it. There was only one woman he was interested in and she wasn't returning his calls or answering when he knocked on her door. He was about ready to show up at the precinct, although turning up at her work was a last resort. But he was almost desperate enough to take that route.

A scent that carried a multitude of memories and fired his senses wrapped around him. He was in bad shape when just thinking about Serena conjured up her scent.

"Oh, shit."

"No, shit."

"Whoa, shit."

Nick turned around to see what had the three stooges so worked up.

Serena. Walking toward him. Almost right behind him. Wearing those boots.

"Serena?" He couldn't quite believe his eyes. Was she really here? He looked at the beer on the table. "You were the lady at the bar?"

"Yeah. Until I got cold feet and had to go to the bathroom." She looked around at AJ, Matt and Tim. "Hi, I'm Serena. Which one of you is AJ?"

AJ stood up and shook her hand. "I'm AJ."

"Nice to meet you. I just wanted to thank you for giving me such a great cover. I'd have been in trouble without your bet."

"You're in trouble now if you're here to see him. But I'm such a nice guy, I'm willing to help you out again. You don't really want Nicky, but me, I'm available." He grinned over his shoulder at Nick.

Nick stared back. "I think your mother's always liked your nose. It'd be a shame if I had to rearrange it for you." Nick was only kidding…well, sort of.

AJ laughed and held out his hands. "It's cool.

Just offering my assistance." He winked at Serena. "Matt and Tim, why don't we check out the dart tournament in the back room?" They all left, casting a few backward glances as they headed to the back.

Nick couldn't quite believe she was really here. He blurted out the first thing that came to mind. "I tried to call you. I went by your house."

"I haven't been at my place. I took a trip. I went home, Nick."

What she'd just said and what it meant slammed him in the gut. "Home home?"

"Yeah. I went to Cleveland. I had to."

"How's your mother?"

"She's good. It was great to see her. I saw my dad also."

"Did you mean to?"

"Of course, I meant to. I had to go to prison to see him."

"How was it?"

"Very liberating."

"How did you find me here?"

"You mentioned this place once in a conversation. You know I *am* a detective. Actually, that's past tense. I quit the force."

His head reeled. She'd quit. "But why? You're good at it and you love it—"

She shook her head, interrupting him. "No. I am good at it, but I never loved it. It was something of a dark compulsion, an obsession. At the suggestion of someone very special, I traded my handcuffs for a hand mixer. I've enrolled in culinary school."

Nick's usual gift for gab had deserted him, leaving him sitting on his stool, speechless. She drew a deep breath, as if preparing for really big news. It'd be damn hard to top what she'd told him so far.

"I was wrong, Nick. I thought I was listening to my gut instinct. But I couldn't actually hear what it was telling me. I'm sorry for the things I said that morning. You're a good man and I believe in that innate goodness. I love you, Nick."

Had she just said she loved him? He hadn't even told her yet about his plan, about Gleeson, and she had found him to tell him she loved him?

She shifted her bag on her shoulder. "You know, we make a pretty good team and since we're both unemployed—"

He finally found his voice. "I'm not unemployed."

Her head whipped up. "You're not?"

"I'm self-employed." He laughed. "Companies pay me to hack into their files now." He took a few minutes to explain what he'd done and the new clients he'd already contracted. He shook his head, still fairly incredulous. "You did just say you loved me, didn't you?"

"I did."

"So, I know these control issues you have. I'm assuming you have a plan?"

"I do."

"I have a plan of my own," he said. "It involves a partnership proposal. What've you got to say to that?"

"I will."

Epilogue

Eighteen months later...

SERENA NEARLY JUMPED OUT of her skin when Nick slid his arms around her from behind. Good thing she wasn't holding a sharp knife in her hands, which was always a distinct possibility in the kitchen at McCaffrey's Diner. She stretched her back and arched her neck as his lips nuzzled the spot behind her ear he referred to as her sweet spot. "When did you get here?"

"Mmmm. I just dropped by. I know late Saturday afternoons are a slow time for you," Nick said, nuzzling her shoulder and sending chills chasing down her spine, his hands cupping the fullness of her belly. "How's my girl today?"

"Which one of us?" She rubbed her enormous stomach and the little vixen inside kicked at her.

"Both of you."

Before she could answer, Big John piped up. "Hey, knock it off. That's how you got my partner in that shape in the first place."

Before she graduated from culinary school, Big

John had offered Serena a partnership in the diner since, as he put it, he wasn't getting any younger and he didn't have any kids of his own to leave it to.

"Yeah, well, you're wearing my wife out. I'm going to make her sit down for a minute to rest and have a glass of orange juice," Nick said. He looked smug today. Maybe he'd signed a new client. Her husband certainly liked to hack into company files and he was damn good at it.

"Wait up. I've got to finish this strudel."

"No. The strudel can wait. You need a break."

He all but shoved her toward the door. "You know, O'Malley, I love you, but being married doesn't mean you can run my life. If you think—"

He actually shoved her through the door and a very large group of people all yelling "Surprise" cut her off in mid-diatribe.

Nick turned to her with a big grin. "You were saying, sweet Serena?"

"What…"

Trixie marched over with an ear-to-ear smile. "You didn't think we were gonna let you have that baby without a shower, did you?"

Serena looked around. All of her boys from the station were there with their wives—thank God, Pantoni and Francesca had worked things out. Nick's mom and dad, as well as Rourke, Portia and her son, Danny, were part of the group. AJ, Matt, Tim and Tim's wife, Marsha, were sitting in a booth. Someone had even set Sheila up in a booth of her own. Probably AJ.

Nick slipped his arm around her waist. "You okay?"

She'd never felt so loved. So surrounded by family. Between this and baby hormones…she'd kill someone if she cried. "Whose idea was this?" she said.

"Do you think it's a good idea or a bad idea?" Nick looked cautious.

She laughed at his goofy expression. He was always making her laugh. She loved this man and these people, and she was fortunate enough that they loved her in return. "Definitely a good idea."

He grinned and winked at her. "Then it was definitely mine."

"Don't make me take out my whip."

"Promise? That'll give me something to look forward to." Ah, that flicker of heat in his eyes that always meant good things for both of them. "If I don't die from waiting."

"Hmm. You'll live. I know how much you like anticipation."

HARLEQUIN *Blaze*

The last book in the
RED LETTER NIGHTS
miniseries is here!

Bree Addison never dreamed that landing in
Lucas Russell's yard would change everything.
Who knew that her rescuer would be bent on
having a sizzling affair with her? And who could
have guessed that her nights would suddenly
become one big sensual adventure?

Only adventures aren't meant to last....

Find out how the story unfolds in
GOING ALL OUT
by *Jeanie London*

Available February 2006 wherever books are sold.

THE WHITE STAR
The quest continues with book #2 of The White Star continuity…

Jamie Wilson thinks his best friend, Marissa
Suarez, is dating the wrong men—his wanting
her for himself has *nothing* to do with his opinion.
When Marissa's apartment suddenly becomes
a target for thieves, Jamie steps up to the plate.
Maybe Marissa will finally see the hidden gem
he is—inside the bedroom and out!

Hidden Gems
by
CARRIE ALEXANDER

*Don't miss out…
this modern-day hunt is like no other!*

HBTWS0206

If you enjoyed what you just read,
then we've got an offer you can't resist!

Take 2 bestselling
love stories FREE!
Plus get a FREE surprise gift!

Clip this page and mail it to Harlequin Reader Service®

IN U.S.A.	IN CANADA
3010 Walden Ave.	P.O. Box 609
P.O. Box 1867	Fort Erie, Ontario
Buffalo, N.Y. 14240-1867	L2A 5X3

YES! Please send me 2 free Harlequin® Blaze™ novels and my free surprise gift. After receiving them, if I don't wish to receive anymore, I can return the shipping statement marked cancel. If I don't cancel, I will receive 6 brand-new novels each month, before they're available in stores! In the U.S.A., bill me at the bargain price of $3.99 plus 25¢ shipping and handling per book and applicable sales tax, if any*. In Canada, bill me at the bargain price of $4.47 plus 25¢ shipping and handling per book and applicable taxes**. That's the complete price and a savings of at least 10% off the cover prices—what a great deal! I understand that accepting the 2 free books and gift places me under no obligation ever to buy any books. I can always return a shipment and cancel at any time. Even if I never buy another book from Harlequin, the 2 free books and gift are mine to keep forever.

151 HDN D7ZZ
351 HDN D72D

Name	(PLEASE PRINT)	
Address	Apt.#	
City	State/Prov.	Zip/Postal Code

Not valid to current Harlequin® Blaze™ subscribers.

Want to try two free books from another series?
Call 1-800-873-8635 or visit www.morefreebooks.com.

* Terms and prices subject to change without notice. Sales tax applicable in N.Y.
** Canadian residents will be charged applicable provincial taxes and GST.
All orders subject to approval. Offer limited to one per household.
® and ™ are registered trademarks owned and used by the trademark owner and/or its licensee.

BLZ05   ©2005 Harlequin Enterprises Limited.

HARLEQUIN®

Blaze™

COMING NEXT MONTH

#231 GOING ALL OUT Jeanie London
Red Letter Nights
Bree Addison never dreamed that landing in Lucas Russell's yard would change everything. Who knew that her rescuer would be bent on having a sizzling affair with her? And who could have guessed that her nights would suddenly become one big sensual adventure? Only, adventures aren't meant to last….

#232 ROOM SERVICE Jill Shalvis
Do Not Disturb
It should be simple. All TV producer Em Harris has to do is convince chef Jacob Hill to sign on for her new culinary show. Only, when she sets foot in Hush, the sex-themed hotel where Jacob works, she knows she's in over her head. Especially when she develops an irresistible craving for the sinfully delicious chef…

#233 TALL, TANNED & TEXAN Kimberly Raye
24 Hours: Island Fling
After years of trying to make cowboy Rance McGraw notice her, Deanie Codge is taking action! Two weeks at Camp E.D.E.N., a notorious island retreat, will teach her to unleash her inner sex kitten. The next time she sees her cowboy, she'll be ready. And it turns out to be sooner than she thinks….

#234 SINFULLY SWEET Janelle Dension, Jacquie D'Alessandro, Kate Hoffmann
A Decadent Valentine's Day Collection
Sex or chocolate. Which is better? This Valentine's Day, join three of Blaze's bestselling authors in proving that, in both sex *and* chocolate, too much of a good thing…is a good thing!

#235 FLIRTATION Samantha Hunter
The HotWires, Bk. 3
EJ Beaumont is one big flirt. Not exactly the best trait for a cop, but it's an asset on his current computer crime investigation. He's flirting big-time with a sexy online psychic who—rumor has it—is running a lonely-hearts scam. Only problem is, as a psychic, Charlotte Gerard has EJ's number but good!

#236 HIDDEN GEMS Carrie Alexander
The White Star, Bk. 2
Jamie Wilson thinks his best friend, Marissa Suarez, is dating the wrong men—his wanting her for himself has *nothing* to do with his opinion. When Marissa's apartment suddenly becomes a target for thieves, Jamie steps up to the plate. Maybe Marissa will finally see the hidden gem he is—inside the bedroom and out!

www.eHarlequin.com

HBCNM0106